THE WORLD OF

CW01500610

Francis Durbridge

WILLIAMS & WHITING

The script in this book was sourced from the
BBC Written Archive Centre
and the transcriptions have been made by the publisher
and have not been checked for accuracy by the BBC.

Cover design by Timo Schroeder

9781912582532

Williams & Whiting (Publishers)
15 Chestnut Grove, Hurstpierpoint,
West Sussex, BN6 9SS

Titles by Francis Durbridge published by Williams & Whiting

1   The Scarf – tv serial
2   Paul Temple and the Curzon Case - radio   serial
3   La Boutique – radio serial
4   The Broken Horseshoe – tv serial
5   Three Plays for Radio Volume 1
6   Send for Paul Temple – radio serial
7   A Time of Day – tv serial
8   Death Comes to The Hibiscus – stage play
     The Essential Heart – radio play
     (writing as Nicholas Vane)
9   Send for Paul Temple – stage play
10 The Teckman Biography – tv serial
11 Paul Temple and Steve – radio serial
12 Twenty Minutes From Rome – a teleplay
13 Portrait of Alison – tv serial
14 Paul Temple: Two Plays for Radio Volume 1
15 Three Plays for Radio Volume 2
16 The Other Man – tv serial
17 Paul Temple and the Spencer Affair – radio   serial
18 Step In The Dark – film script
19 My Friend Charles – tv serial
20 A Case For Paul Temple – radio serial
21 Murder In The Media – more rediscovered serials and
     stories
22 The Desperate People – tv serial
23 Paul Temple: Two Plays for Television
24 And Anthony Sherwood Laughed – radio series

Murder At The Weekend – the rediscovered newspaper serials
and short stories

Titles by Francis Durbridge to be published by Williams & Whiting

A Game of Murder
A Man Called Harry Brent
Bat Out of Hell
Breakaway – The Family Affair
Breakaway – The Local Affair
Farewell Leicester Square
Five Minute Mysteries (includes Michael Starr Investigates and The Memoirs of Andre d'Arnell)
Johnny Washington Esquire
Melissa
Mr Hartington Died Tomorrow
Murder On The Continent (Further re-discovered serials and stories)
One Man To Another – a novel
Operation Diplomat
Paul Temple and the Alex Affair
Paul Temple and the Canterbury Case (film script)
Paul Temple and the Conrad Case
Paul Temple and the Geneva Mystery
Paul Temple and the Gilbert Case
Paul Temple and the Gregory Affair
Paul Temple and the Jonathan Mystery
Paul Temple and the Lawrence Affair
Paul Temple and the Madison Mystery
Paul Temple and the Margo Mystery
Paul Temple and the Sullivan Mystery
Paul Temple and the Vandyke Affair
Paul Temple Intervenes
Paul Temple: Two Plays For Radio Vol 2 (Send For Paul Temple and News of Paul Temple)
Send For Paul Temple Again

The Doll

The Female of the Species (The Girl from the Hibiscus and Introducing Gail Carlton)

The Man From Washington

The Passenger

Tim Frazer and the Salinger Affair

Tim Frazer and the Mellin Forrest Mystery

INTRODUCTION

Francis Durbridge (1912-98) was the foremost writer of mystery thrillers for BBC radio from the 1930s to the 1960s. As early as 1938 he found the niche in which he was to establish his name, when his serial *Send for Paul Temple* was so successful that it resulted in numerous sequels that built an impressive UK and European fanbase. So it was entirely natural that, while continuing to write for radio, he should move into the newer medium of television – with the result that in 1952 *The Broken Horseshoe* became the first thriller serial on BBC Television.

The World of Tim Frazer was Durbridge's ninth television serial, first transmitted on 15 November 1960. His previous eight serials had each consisted of six thirty-minute episodes, but this one ran for eighteen thirty-minute episodes covering three stories, transmitted from 15 November 1960 to 14 March 1961. This made it the longest serial at that time transmitted by BBC Television, and it qualified as continuous by using the audience-holding technique of a cliff-hanger ending to each episode but with the changeover in stories taking place during episodes seven and thirteen. Although Durbridge originally planned to use the title *The World of David Marquand*, the change to Tim Frazer cemented the latter's place in television history.

This first Tim Frazer serial was written jointly with Clive Exton, and Frazer was a very different character from radio's Paul Temple – an ordinary man lacking Temple's sophistication, and with no intention of becoming a detective until drawn into the counter-espionage game. The producer/director was Alan Bromly, who had been responsible for every Durbridge television serial from *Portrait of Alison* in 1955, and although the other two stories in the Tim Frazer sequence were in the hands of other directors Bromly afterwards returned to direct five more Durbridge serials until *Bat Out of Hell* (1966).

The team of Durbridge and Bromly always provided the familiar ingredients – red herrings galore, cliff-hangers to end each episode, and the certainty that viewers should not believe anything that anyone says. Consequently Durbridge became recognised as the pre-eminent exponent of the television thriller, the master of twisting plots following the tortuous trail of a character struggling in a vicious web spun by a killer who remained concealed until the final episode. Indeed his popularity was uniquely rewarded by the BBC, as all his television serials from *The World of Tim Frazer* onwards received the unprecedented accolade of the screen credit "Francis Durbridge Presents" before the title sequence of each episode.

All three inter-linked Tim Frazer serials featured superb performances by Jack Hedley (1929-2021) as Tim and Ralph Michael (1907-94) as his spymaster Charles Ross. Hedley had been a regular television actor from the 1950s, but usually in small parts until his role as Tim Frazer catapulted him to fame and led to film and television successes – including Hammer Films' *The Scarlet Blade* (1963) and *The Anniversary* (1968), television's *Colditz* (1972-74) and *Who Pays the Ferryman?* (1977), and the James Bond movie *For Your Eyes Only* (1981). His Durbridge credentials were also significant, as he appeared in the *Paul Temple* television series (*Murder in Munich*, 12 and 19 July 1970) and was also the leading man in the 1983 countrywide tour of Durbridge's stage play *Nightcap*.

But it is impossible to resist mentioning the charismatic Brian Wilde (1927-2008), who played Tupper in *The World of Tim Frazer* long before his acclaimed comedy runs as Prison Officer Barrowclough in *Porridge* (1974-77) and Foggy Dewhurst in *Last of the Summer Wine* (1976-97). He had already played a major role in Durbridge's *Portrait of Alison* (1955) and went on to become a Durbridge regular after *The World of Tim Frazer* in *Melissa* (1964) and *A Man Called Harry Brent* (1965).

Durbridge's television serials had an element of "Britishness", distinguishing them from "sock-in-the-jaw" American imports that dominated UK television at the time, and perhaps because of this he acquired an enthusiastic following in Europe. Already his radio serials had been broadcast in various countries from the late 1930s, in translation and using their own actors; then beginning with *The Other Man* (1959 in Germany as *Der Andere*) there followed European versions that attracted a large body of viewers. So addictive was Francis Durbridge that German commentators defined his serials as *straßenfeger* (street sweepers), because so many people stayed at home to listen to them on the radio or watch them on television.

In the case of *The World of Tim Frazer*, European television companies produced the three Frazer serials separately – with the German version *Tim Frazer* (14 – 25 January 1963, six episodes) translated by Marianne de Barde and directed by Hans Quest; and the Italian version *Traffico d'armi nel golfo* (12 – 26 November 1977, three episodes) translated by Franca Cancogni, adapted by Aurelio Chiesa and directed by Leonardo Cortese. Although the first two Frazer serials appeared on German television in 1963 and 1964, it was not until 1971 that a production of the third serial was seen in Germany – *Das Messer* (30 November – 4 December 1971, three episodes), translated by Marianne de Barde and directed by the legendary Rolf von Sydow.

As with many of Francis Durbridge's radio and television scripts, *The World of Tim Frazer* was novelised – with each of the three serials becoming a separate book, all published by Hodder & Stoughton. *The World of Tim Frazer* (Hodder &

Stoughton, January 1962) was also published in the US in August 1962 by Dodd, Mead. In Germany it appeared as *Tim Frazer*, in France as *Où est passé Harry?* and in the Netherlands as *De wereld van Tim Frazer*. For UK lovers of audiobooks, it was marketed in eight audiocassettes and six CDs, read by Clive Mantle, by BBC Audio in 2009; and later, in two CDs, there was an abridged reading by Anthony Head marketed by AudioGO in 2010.

Melvyn Barnes
Author of *Francis Durbridge: The Complete Guide* (Williams & Whiting, 2018)

This book reproduces Francis Durbridge's original script together with the list of characters and actors of the BBC programme on the dates mentioned, but the eventual broadcast might have edited Durbridge's script in respect of scenes, dialogue and character names.

THE WORLD OF TIM FRAZER

A serial in seven episodes
By FRANCIS DURBRIDGE
And CLIVE EXTON
Broadcast on BBC Television
15 November – 27 December 1960
CAST:

Tim Frazer . . . . Jack Hedley
Norman Gibson . . . . .Fred Ferris
Madge Gibson . . . . Karal Gardner
Crombie . . . . Donald Morley
Dr Killick . . . . .Gerald Cross
P.C. Muir . . . . .Frank Pettitt
Captain Nikiyan . . . . .Steve Plytas
Mrs Glover . . . . .Ann Way
Helen Baker . . . . Heather Chasen
Charles Ross . . . . .Ralph Michael
Hobson . . . . .Alan Rolfe
Anya . . . . Janina Faye
Ruth Edwards . . . . .Barbara Couper
Donald Edwards . . . . . . Redmond Phillips
Tupper . . . . Brian Wilde
Caxton . . . . Maurice Durant
Army private . . . . .Neil Hunter
Projectionist . . . . .Donald Pelmear
Harry Denston . . . . .John Dearth
Ma Dodsworth . . . . .Vi Stevens
Lester . . . . .Peter Hammond
Shop-keeper . . . . Arthur R. Webb
Police Sergeant . . . . Frank Sieman
Police Constable . . . . . . Anthony Wingate

Dr Harris . . . . Dennis Edwards
Will . . . . Jack Rodney
Walters . . . . Christopher Rhodes

Episode One

OPEN TO: The harbour at Henton, a north country fishing village. The sea is rough and the wind is blowing. We are outside the village inn – The Three Bells.

CUT TO: The Saloon Bar-cum-Lounge of The Three Bells. The bar has oak beams, bench tables and chairs and an entrance from the street. There is a door to the kitchen and a staircase to the upstairs rooms.

NORMAN GIBSON, the landlord, is behind the bar, polishing glasses. He is a rotund, pleasant direct man in his middle fifties. TIM FRAZER sits at the end of the bar, reading a book – a glass of beer in front of him. FRAZER is a serious looking man in his late thirties. He is wearing sports trousers and a sweater. NORMAN glances across at him.

NORMAN: Wind hasn't dropped then.

FRAZER: No, it certainly hasn't.

NORMAN: Thought it was going to this afternoon.

FRAZER: Yes, so did I.

FRAZER stares at the window for a moment and then goes back to his book. MADGE GIBSON, the landlord's daughter, comes down the staircase. She is carrying a basin of water.

NORMAN: How is he?

MADGE: No better.

MADGE shakes her head at him. She goes behind the bar and empties the basin into the sink under it. She notices FRAZER.

MADGE: Have a good walk this afternoon, Mr Frazer?

FRAZER: Oh – yes, thanks, Madge. I got as far as the quay.

MADGE: Didn't choose much of a day for it.

FRAZER: No, but I enjoyed it.

3

After a slight pause.

FRAZER: How's the patient?

MADGE: Dr Killick doesn't hold out much hope, I'm afraid.

FRAZER: Is the doctor still with him?

MADGE: Yes. He'll be down in a minute. He wants a word with you, Mr Frazer.

FRAZER nods.

MADGE: The doctor says he doubts whether he'll last the night.

NORMAN: He hasn't come round again?

MADGE: No, not since last night.

NORMAN: Oh dear, poor chap. You know, it's a terrible thing – it really is. (*Shaking his head*) I just can't get over it. Poor devil …

The door from the street opens, letting in a gust of wind. ARTHUR CROMBIE enters, shutting the door behind him. CROMBIE is in his early fifties; has an untidy moustache and nicotined fingers. He is a commercial traveller. He carries a suitcase and a battered briefcase. He is tired and evidently fed-up.

CROMBIE: Good Heavens above. What weather!

NORMAN: Evening, sir. What can I do for you?

CROMBIE: Good evening. You the landlord?

NORMAN: That's right, sir. Gibson's the name.

CROMBIE: Well, I'd like a room, old man. (*Surveying the bar*) That is, if you've got any rooms?

NORMAN: Just for the one night?

CROMBIE: Yes. Possibly two; but I hope not. Had a bit of a bust-up with the car.

NORMAN: Well, we can do that for you all right, sir.

CROMBIE: (*Taking off his raincoat*) Oh, good! Splendid! Now all I need is a stiff Scotch.

NORMAN: Right, sir. Anything with it, sir?

4

NORMAN pours the drink.

CROMBIE: No fear! Will you join me?

NORMAN: Very kind of you, sir. I'll have a beer, if I may.

CROMBIE: Whatever you feel like, old man. Oh, by the way, have you a phone I could use?

NORMAN: Well …

MADGE: (*Nodding towards the telephone behind the bar*) We would have usually, sir, but it's out of order at the moment. Lines blown down.

CROMBIE: Oh, damn! That's all I need!

NORMAN puts the drinks on the bar.

CROMBIE: What do I owe you?

NORMAN: Three shillings, if you please, sir.

CROMBIE nods, puts the money on the bar, and then raises his glass to NORMAN.

CROMBIE: Cheerio …

NORMAN: (*Drinking*) Cheers, sir.

They drink.

CROMBIE: By George, you get some pretty rough weather in these parts!

NORMAN: It's an improvement on last week.

CROMBIE: What did you have last week – a typhoon?

NORMAN: (*Laughing*) It certainly felt like it at times – didn't it, Mr Frazer?

FRAZER looks up and gives a friendly nod of confirmation. CROMBIE looks at FRAZER; it is apparently the first time he has noticed him.

CROMBIE: Good evening.

MADGE: Didn't you read about the Russians?

CROMBIE: Russians? (*Suddenly*) Oh, that was in this part of the world, was it?

5

NORMAN: Yes, just outside the harbour – practically on our doorstep. (*Shaking his head*) Worst storm I remember in thirty years.

CROMBIE: (*Smiling*) It's always thirty years!

NORMAN: (*Laughing*) You should have had a basinful!

CROMBIE: (*To MADGE*) Yes, I remember reading about that Russian ship. But what happened exactly? Did they get the men off all right?

MADGE: They rescued most of the crew, but two were drowned – swept away.

NORMAN: It's a miracle any of 'em were saved, if you ask me.

CROMBIE: Where are they – the ones that were rescued?

NORMAN: In the cottage hospital. Although as a matter of fact we've got one of 'em here. (*Points upstairs*)

CROMBIE: Really? How did that happen?

NORMAN: They had to bring three or four of them here while the rescue work was going on. This chap – Anstrov – was too ill to move. The doctor wouldn't hear of it.

CROMBIE: He must have been pretty bad.

NORMAN: He was and still is, poor chap. Touch and go. He was in the water for hours, and at this time of year.

CROMBIE: Poor devil. What an experience!

MADGE goes off to the kitchen. CROMBIE drinks then looks across at FRAZER who is still reading his book.

CROMBIE: Were you down here last week, sir?

FRAZER: (*Looking up*) Yes, I was.

CROMBIE: Must have been very exciting – I mean, the storm, and everything?

FRAZER: Yes, very exciting. (*He looks at his book*)

6

NORMAN: Mr Frazer went out with a rescue party. (*Smiles at FRAZER*) Was very nearly swept overboard.

CROMBIE: Go on? Is that so?

FRAZER looks up again.

CROMBIE: Crombie's my name, sir. Arthur Crombie. I'm from Leeds. Textiles.

FRAZER: (*Politely*) Mr Crombie … Are you just passing through?

CROMBIE: No; no, had a bit of a smash-up with the car, that's why I'm here.

FRAZER: Oh, really?

CROMBIE: (*Nodding*) Picked an argument with a lorry. Damn fool thing to do.

FRAZER closes his book and takes an interest in what CROMBIE is saying.

FRAZER: Where was this?

CROMBIE: On the main road, just coming into the village. Took the corner too sharp and went bang slap into a whacking big lorry.

FRAZER: Lucky you weren't hurt.

CROMBIE: Damn lucky. Lucky no one was hurt. Made an awful mess of the car though. Don't know how the Dickens I'm going to get to Nottingham tomorrow; that's my worry.

FRAZER smiles and moves away from the bar.

CROMBIE: (*To FRAZER*) Oh – won't you have a drink, old man?

FRAZER: Not at the moment, thank you.

FRAZER goes up the staircase to his room. MADGE returns from the kitchen with a plate of sandwiches which she places on the bar.

MADGE: Been getting to know our Mr Frazer?

CROMBIE:	What? Oh – had a bit of a chat, you know. (*Picking up one of the sandwiches*) Has he been here long?
MADGE:	Just over a week, isn't it, dad?
NORMAN:	Who's this? Mr Frazer?
MADGE:	Yes.
NORMAN:	Week yesterday. Nice chap – but very quiet. Keeps himself to himself as you might say. (*Glancing at MADGE*) Not that that's a bad thing at times.
CROMBIE:	What's he doing up here – on holiday? (*He starts on the sandwich*)
NORMAN:	No – he came up here to meet a friend of his – Denston I think he said they called him. Yes, that's right. Harry Denston.
CROMBIE:	What happened?
NORMAN:	The chap didn't turn up.
MADGE:	They used to be in business together.
CROMBIE:	Frazer and this chap Denston?
NORMAN:	That's right. I think it was an engineering business and they went bust or something. I'm not really sure.

DR KILLICK comes down the staircase. He is a small bald-headed man of about fifty, dressed in a rather crumpled lounge suit. He crosses over to the bar.

MADGE:	Any news, Doctor?
KILLICK:	Nothing new, I'm afraid. It's only a question of time now. I shall be surprised if he lasts the night.

KILLICK sits on a bar stool.

MADGE:	Oh, Doctor!
KILLICK:	Well, we've done all we can, Madge. We can't do any more.
NORMAN:	He hasn't come round at all?

8

KILLICK: No. I've given him an injection and, frankly, I hope he doesn't come round. He's better off as he is.

CROMBIE: Good evening. Nasty business.

NORMAN: I expect you could do with a drink, doctor?

KILLICK: Well – yes, I could, as a matter of fact. A Scotch if you please.

NORMAN starts to pour the drink.

KILLICK: I'm only sorry it had to happen here. (*He smiles at MADGE*) Although I could scarcely have had a more professional assistant –

MADGE: How are all the others, doctor – the ones at the hospital?

KILLICK: Well, one of them died, as you know. The rest of them are doing well. Just shock – most of them. The First Mate and some of the others are being discharged tomorrow morning.

NORMAN: Oh good.

CROMBIE: Do you think I could have another Scotch?

NORMAN: Why, yes, of course, sir. Sorry, Mr Crombie.

DR KILLICK looks at CROMBIE, then turns as FRAZER comes down the staircase.

FRAZER: Good evening, doctor!

KILLICK: Hello, Mr Frazer!

FRAZER: (*Crossing to the bar*) I understand you'd like a word with me?

KILLICK: Yes, I would, if you can spare a moment. Will you have a drink?

FRAZER: Not just now, thanks.

KILLICK: It's about last night.

FRAZER: Oh – yes. Madge told you about that, did she?

KILLICK: Yes, but I'd like to hear your version of it because both the Captain and the First Mate keep bothering me about Anstrov.

FRAZER: Well – there's very little to tell. Madge knocked me up last night, just as I was getting ready for bed, and asked me to go along and see Anstrov. (*He smiles at MADGE*) She was a bit upset, I think.

MADGE: It was silly, really, but I'd been sitting with him all evening and then suddenly, he opened his eyes and started talking.

KILLICK: In Russian, I suppose?

MADGE: I suppose so. Anyway, I couldn't make head nor tail of it, and he was getting sort of frantic, so I knocked up Mr Frazer – he's in the next room, you see. Dad was still closing up the bar, so I didn't want to disturb him.

KILLICK: (*To FRAZER*) Madge tells me that Anstrov was still talking when you saw him – she said you seemed to understand what he was saying.

FRAZER: That's right.

KILLICK: (*A shade surprised*) You speak Russian, then?

FRAZER: Yes, I do. Not frightfully well – but I understand it all right.

KILLICK: Did Anstrov say anything – anything intelligible, I mean?

FRAZER: No – not really. He was delirious. The only thing that made sense was that he kept calling for someone – someone called Anya.

KILLICK:	Anna?
FRAZER:	No – Anya. (*A shrug*) His wife, or girlfriend, I imagine.
KILLICK:	And that's all?
FRAZER:	I'm afraid so.
KILLICK:	Well, thank you, Mr Frazer. I'll tell the Captain what happened. (*He finishes his drink*) Now if you'll excuse me, I'll take another look at my patient before I go.

KILLICK turns and leaves the bar and goes up the staircase. As he does so the telephone at the end of the bar rings. MADGE picks up the receiver.

MADGE:	Hello?
OPERATOR:	(*On the other end of the line*) Henton 317?
MADGE:	Yes, speaking.
OPERATOR:	Your line's all right now – it's back in service.
MADGE:	Thank you.

MADGE replaces the receiver and then looks across at CROMBIE.

MADGE:	The phone's working again now, Mr Crombie – if you want to make a call.
CROMBIE:	(*As he finishes his drink*) Oh, good!

CUT TO:	The Saloon Bar of The Three Bells. Day.

FRAZER is sitting at a table. PC MUIR is facing him. On the table is a collection of articles: wallet, watch, comb, tie-pin, notebook, lighter. All crumpled and sea stained. MUIR is making out a list as FRAZER reads them out to him.

FRAZER:	One tie pin.
MUIR:	(*Writing*) One tie-pin.
FRAZER:	One wristwatch.
MUIR:	One wristwatch.
FRAZER:	One comb.

11

MUIR:	One comb. One chromium-plated cigarette lighter … one pair of cufflinks.
FRAZER:	(*Sitting back*) And that's the lot?
MUIR:	Yes. Not much, is it?
FRAZER:	No. What happens to these things?
MUIR:	I dunno. The Russian captain's coming down later. I suppose we hand them over to him for the next of kin.

CROMBIE comes down the stairs carrying his suitcase and with his raincoat over his arm.

CROMBIE:	Been any phone calls for me this morning?
FRAZER:	Not that I know of.
CROMBIE:	Oh, damn and blast! That ruddy garage swore they'd give me a ring! (*Indicating the things on the table*) They the Russki's things?
MUIR:	That's right, sir.
CROMBIE:	Fancy dying in a dead-and-alive hole like this! Bad enough living here, I should think. (*He dismisses the subject*) Seen the landlord about?
FRAZER:	Gibson? He's gone into Henton to meet his wife off the London train.
MUIR:	Mrs Gibson's been visiting her married sister down in London.
CROMBIE:	What about the daughter?
MUIR:	She's out shopping. Said she'd be back in about an hour.
CROMBIE:	Oh, blast! Well, since you seem to be the expert on local news, Constable, perhaps you could tell me what I do about paying my bill?
MUIR:	Certainly, sir. Mr Gibson left it on the bar, in case you wanted to settle up.

CROMBIE goes to the bar and picks up his bill. As he does so the street door opens and DR KILLICK enters escorting CAPTAIN SERGE NIKIYAN. He is a big, fair man about forty-five. He wears a reefer jacket and walks with the aid of a stick.

KILLICK: Ah, Muir, good morning! This is Captain Nikiyan. He's come to collect Anstrov's belongings.

MUIR: Yes, sir – I've got them all here. We've made out a list, if the Captain would be good enough to sign for them.

KILLICK: (*Showing the article to NIKIYAN*) Those are Anstrov's things, Captain.

NIKIYAN: Thank you, yes.

MUIR: (*Giving him a pen*) If you'd just sign for them, sir.

NIKIYAN does so. MUIR collects the things together and passes them to NIKIYAN. As he does so a large ticket falls from amongst them. FRAZER stoops and picks it up and looks at it.

FRAZER: (*Looking at the card*) This isn't Anstrov's …

MUIR: What is it, sir?

FRAZER: It's a garage ticket.

MUIR: What do you mean, sir – a garage ticket?

FRAZER: You know – the sort of thing you get when you leave your car. A receipt, if you like.

MUIR: (*Looking at the paper in FRAZER's hand*) Brompton Road Garage, London, SW7 …

NIKIYAN: Anstrov never in London …

MUIR: Well, it came out of his room all right. Brought it down meself.

13

FRAZER: It must belong to the landlord or one of the previous guests. I'll give it to him when he comes in.

FRAZER takes out his wallet and puts the receipt in and returns the wallet to his pocket.

FRAZER: Captain, the night before Anstrov died, he was conscious for a few minutes. I don't know if the doctor told you this?

KILLICK: No, I haven't not yet. Go ahead, Frazer, and tell him what happened …

FRAZER: (*To NIKIYAN*) Well – I went in to Anstrov and he spoke a few words. All I could make out was that he was calling for someone – someone called "Anya". That's all, I'm afraid. I thought his family might like to know that.

NIKIYAN: (*Thoughtfully*) Anya? That is perhaps his friend? His – what is it you? – fiancée?

FRAZER: Well, I wouldn't know …

NIKIYAN: (*Nodding*) He was to marry a girl from Kiev. Anya is perhaps her name.

FRAZER: Well, yes – I imagine it was something like that.

NIKIYAN: (*A sigh and a shrug*) There is nothing we can do now. It is too late.

MUIR: Yes, well – Dr Killick did everything he could, Captain. He even went to the trouble of …

NIKIYAN: (*Interrupting him*) Da! Da! (*Smiling at KILLICK*) He has been most kind. I wish to thank all of you for your kindness. You have been very good to us. All of you.

NIKIYAN shakes hands, very formally, with all of them in turn, saying to each as he does so: "I thank you".

14

KILLICK: Shall we go, Captain?

KILLICK leads NIKIYAN to the door and they go out.
CROMBIE looks down at his hand which was shaken by
NIKIYAN.

CROMBIE: Extraordinary chap.

CUT TO: Outside The Three Bells.

DR KILLICK and CAPTAIN NIKIYAN come out of the pub
and walk away.

CUT TO: The Saloon Bar of the Three Bells. Night.

FRAZER is at one of the tables finishing his supper and
writing notes on a pad at the same time. MADGE is behind
the bar. NORMAN comes down the staircase and crosses to
FRAZER.

NORMAN: Your friend got off all right then, Mr
               Frazer?

FRAZER: My friend? Oh – Crombie? Yes – he got off
               just before lunch. I'm off tomorrow too, by
               the way. I want to catch the nine o'clock
               from Henton.

NORMAN: (*Sitting down opposite FRAZER*) Oh, what a
               pity – just as we was getting to know you,
               like.

FRAZER: (*Indicating the note that he's just written*) I
               was just writing a telegram. I'll phone it
               through from here.

NORMAN takes the note from FRAZER.

NORMAN: I'll get Madge to do it now – if that's all
               right?

FRAZER: Oh, I can do it.

NORMAN: No – you finish your supper in peace. (*He*
               calls across to MADGE) Madge!

MADGE comes over from behind the bar.

15

NORMAN: Just phone this telegram through for Mr
            Frazer, will you? (*He hands MADGE the
            paper*)
FRAZER: The address is on the top.
MADGE: (*Reading*) "Miss Helen Baker, Shaftesbury
            Theatre" … Oh, Mr Frazer, is that <u>the</u> Helen
            Baker?
FRAZER: The actress? Yes …
MADGE: (*Excited*) Oh, Dad – you remember, we saw
            her in that film when we went down to
            Leeds about a month ago.
NORMAN: Oh, aye. I remember.
MADGE: She was lovely. Ever so glamorous. Is she a
            friend of yours, Mr Frazer?
FRAZER: Well, she's engaged to a friend of mine.
NORMAN: Now you just get that telegram sent off and
            mind your own business.
FRAZER: (*Laughing*) Can you read it, Madge?
MADGE: I think so. (*Reading*) "Returning tomorrow.
            No sign of Harry … Tim".
FRAZER: (*Nodding*) That's it.
MADGE crosses to the telephone.
NORMAN: (*Smiling*) These girls! (*Rises*) Well, I'm
            sorry you're leaving us, Mr Frazer.
FRAZER: Yes; so am I. I like it up here. (*Suddenly:
            feeling in his pocket for his wallet*) Oh – by
            the way – there was a garage ticket mixed
            up with Anstrov's things.
NORMAN: A garage ticket?
FRAZER: Yes. It couldn't have been his – it was from
            a London garage. (*Still searching for his
            wallet*) The constable brought it down with
            the other things.
FRAZER cannot find the wallet. He looks at NORMAN.

FRAZER: That's very funny – my wallet's gone.

CUT TO: A Mews in Knightsbridge. Day.
A taxi draws up in front of the house and FRAZER gets out.
He pays the driver, takes a suitcase from the taxi and turns
towards the door of the house.

CUT TO: TIM FRAZER's Drawing Room. Day.
MRS GLOVER looks out of the window.

CUT TO: The Hall of TIM FRAZER's Flat. Day.
TIM FRAZER enters the door. MRS GLOVER comes out to
meet him.

FRAZER: Hello, Mrs Glover! What are you doing
        here?

MRS GLOVER: Miss Baker said you was coming back
        today, so I thought I'd just pop in and
        brighten the place up a bit.

FRAZER: (*Picking up the letters and glancing at*
        the postmarks) Well, that's very
        thoughtful of you, Mrs Glover. I
        appreciate it. (*He smiles at her*) Are there
        any messages?

They go through to the drawing room.

MRS GLOVER: Yes – a Mr Ross telephoned about ten
        minutes ago.

FRAZER: Ross?

MRS GLOVER: Yes. He said you didn't know him, sir, -
        but he'd phone again later.

FRAZER: (*Dismissing the matter*) Oh, I see.

The doorbell rings. FRAZER turns and looks towards the
hall.

MRS GLOVER: That'll be Miss Baker. She said she'd
        drop in on the way to the theatre.

MRS GLOVER goes out into the hall and FRAZER crosses towards the drinks table near the fireplace. He is helping himself to a drink when MRS GLOVER returns with HELEN BAKER. HELEN is an attractive, self-possessed woman in her early thirties.

MRS GLOVER: Miss Baker, sir.

FRAZER: (*Turning*) Hello, Helen – how are you?

HELEN: Darling, how nice to see you!

FRAZER crosses and kisses HELEN on the cheek.

MRS GLOVER: I'll say goodbye, Mr Frazer.

FRAZER: Goodbye, Mrs Glover – and thank you.

MRS GLOVER: Goodbye, Miss Baker.

HELEN: Goodbye, Mrs Glover.

MRS GLOVER goes out into the hall.

HELEN: Well, Tim – how are you?

FRAZER: Oh, I'm all right, Helen, would you like a drink?

HELEN: No, thanks. I'd better not before the show.

FRAZER: Do you mind if I do?

HELEN: No, of course not.

FRAZER finishes mixing himself the drink. HELEN watches him for a moment.

HELEN: So he didn't turn up?

FRAZER: No.

HELEN: Tim, I'm sorry.

FRAZER: There's nothing for you to be sorry about.

HELEN: But I feel responsible. Every penny you had was in that wretched firm.

FRAZER: A slight exaggeration, Helen.

HELEN: Nevertheless – I should have warned you about Harry. I should have warned you about him when we first met.

18

FRAZER:	I don't think he'd have liked it very much.
HELEN:	No, darling – I'm serious. Tim, how much did you lose? Ten thousand? Twelve?
FRAZER:	No; good gracious, nothing like that.
HELEN:	But you must have lost at least –
FRAZER:	Helen, there's no point in going all over this again. I've got no one to blame but myself. When Harry started neglecting the business and going off on those trips of his I should have had it out with him.
HELEN:	You did have it out with him and all you got was a lot of smooth talk. Look at that letter he wrote you. "Meet me in Henton – our troubles are over." I knew perfectly well he wouldn't turn up.
FRAZER:	You seem to forget, Helen, the firm was doing very well until –
HELEN:	Until Harry messed the whole thing up – like he always does. I know.
FRAZER:	Poor Helen!
HELEN:	Poor Helen, nothing! Poor Tim!
FRAZER:	(*Shaking his head*) You've been far more upset about this than I have.
HELEN:	Yes, well – you're not in love with the gentleman!
FRAZER:	I suppose you haven't heard from him?
HELEN:	Not a word – not even a postcard. But he'll turn up. I know Harry. It's all happened before. Tim, what are you going to do now? Are you going to start up again, on your own?
FRAZER:	No. I've learned my lesson. I shall probably try and get a job with one of the big outfits. I may even go abroad.

The telephone rings.

FRAZER: (*Moving towards the phone*) Excuse me. (*Picks up the receiver*) Hello?

The voice of CHARLES ROSS is heard on the other end of the phone.

ROSS: Mr Frazer?

FRAZER: Speaking …

ROSS: Oh – good evening. My name is Ross.

FRAZER: Oh, yes. You telephoned earlier.

ROSS: That's right, I did. I'm sorry if I've disturbed you.

FRAZER: No, that's all right. What can I do for you?

ROSS: Well – I hope you don't think it's an impertinence, Mr Frazer, but I heard about your company going into liquidation, and I wondered if you – yourself – had any future plans?

FRAZER: Well – no, I haven't. (*Vaguely*) I was thinking of going abroad …

ROSS: Oh, I see. Well, if you change your mind and stay over here, get in touch with me. My company could use a man with your qualifications.

FRAZER: (*Pleasantly surprised*) Well – thank you very much. Perhaps you'd tell me the name of your firm and give me your phone number?

ROSS: Yes, certainly. Our number is … (*Pleasantly, apparently changing his mind*) But look, why don't you drop in and see me, anyway? I'd be delighted to meet you.

FRAZER: That's very kind of you.

ROSS: Would tomorrow afternoon be convenient?

FRAZER: Yes – I think so. Three o'clock?

ROSS: That'll suit me admirably. Our address is 29 Moulton Square.

FRAZER: (*Making a note*) 29 … Moulton Square … Thank you, Mr Ross.

ROSS: Not at all. Thank you, Mr Frazer. Three o'clock, then. (*The sound of the receiver being replaced*)

CUT TO: The Corridor of ROSS's Office. Day.

HOBSON knocks on the office door.

CUT TO: The Library at 29 Moulton Square, London, SW1. Day.

The room is a comfortable one, well carpeted, and with antique furniture. Behind the desk sits CHARLES ROSS; a shrewd, intelligent looking man in his early fifties. He is looking through a sheaf of papers.

There is a knock at the door. ROSS, unhurried, opens a drawer in his desk and puts the papers inside.

ROSS: Come in!

The door opens and HOBSON enters. He is a precise, soberly dressed little man of about sixty. He closes the door behind him, crosses to the desk, and places a file in front of ROSS.

HOBSON: Mr Frazer's here, sir.

ROSS: Good. Show him straight in, will you?

HOBSON: Yes, sir. You haven't forgotten your appointment with the Minister?

ROSS: (*Looking at the diary on his desk*) That's at four-thirty, just before the Foreign Office meeting?

HOBSON: Yes, sir.

ROSS: No, that's all right, Hobson.

21

HOBSON moves away from the desk. ROSS nods and HOBSON goes out. ROSS glances at the contents of the file, and after a moment the door opens again and HOBSON returns with FRAZER.

HOBSON: Mr Frazer, sir.

HOBSON goes out, closing the door behind him. FRAZER advances into the room. ROSS stands up to greet him.

FRAZER: Mr Ross?

ROSS: That's right. How very nice of you to come. (*Indicating a chair*) Do sit down.

FRAZER sits in the chair facing ROSS.

ROSS: (*Offering a cigarette box*) Do you smoke, Mr Frazer?

FRAZER: Yes – but I won't at the moment, if you don't mind.

ROSS: As you please.

During the following dialogue ROSS takes a cigarette from the box on the desk and fits it into his cigarette holder.

ROSS: I was sorry to hear about your company. You must have had some very bad luck.

FRAZER: We certainly had our share.

ROSS takes out his lighter, flicks it, and lights his cigarette.

ROSS: (*Looking at the cigarette*) I've got a proposition to put to you, Mr Frazer. It's rather an unusual one, but I think you'll find it interesting. (*Smiling*) At least, I hope so. (*He puts the cigarette lighter in his pocket*) However, let me explain. I'm in charge of a Government department …

FRAZER: (*Surprised*) A Government department?

ROSS: (*Smiling*) Yes … Mr Frazer, you were recently in partnership with a man called Harry Denston. Apart from your business

22

	arrangement, I believe Denston borrowed money from you from time to time?
FRAZER:	Yes, he did – but how do you know that?
ROSS:	(*Flicking open the file on the desk*) If my information's correct, he owes you – personally, not your company … (*Glancing at the file*) Five thousand, seven hundred and twenty pounds …
FRAZER:	Plus forty-one …
ROSS:	(*Quietly; obviously puzzled*) Plus forty-one?
FRAZER:	Yes. Ten days ago I had a letter from Harry asking me to meet him at a place called Henton. The letter implied that he was going to pay me the money he owed me. (*A shrug*) He didn't turn up and to crown it all I had my wallet stolen. There was forty-one pounds in it.
ROSS:	(*Smiling*) Ah, yes! Yes, I see what you mean!
FRAZER:	(*Irritated*) It was a damn nice wallet, too.

ROSS takes FRAZER's wallet out of his inside pocket and places it on the desk.

ROSS:	It was indeed, Mr Frazer. I've been admiring it.

FRAZER rises, staring at the wallet in amazement. He looks at ROSS, who is watching him.

ROSS:	I think you'll find the contents quite in order.
FRAZER:	(*Picking up his wallet*) Look, what the hell is this? Who are you? What is this proposition you're offering me?
CROMBIE:	We want you to find Harry Denston for us.

FRAZER quickly turns and sees CROMBIE who is standing just inside the door. He is considerably smartened-up since

23

we saw him last. He now wears a town suit. His manner too has changed – the "old man" act has vanished.

ROSS: I think you know Crombie. He's a colleague of mine.

FRAZER: Colleague?

ROSS: Yes – we work together in this department.

CROMBIE smiles and moves towards FRAZER.

CROMBIE: I'm sorry I had to take your wallet. I trust it didn't inconvenience you?

FRAZER stares at CROMBIE for a moment, then looks at ROSS.

FRAZER: Why did you get me here this afternoon?

ROSS: I've told you why. I'm offering you a job. (*Quietly*) We want you to find Harry Denston for us.

FRAZER: But Harry hasn't disappeared – he's just gone off somewhere. This often happens! It happened all the time when we were in business together. He'll turn up sooner or later.

ROSS: (*Seriously*) We don't want him sooner or later – we want him now.

FRAZER looks at Ross; after a moment he sits on the arm of the chair.

FRAZER: Have you tried to find Harry?

ROSS: No.

FRAZER: Why not?

ROSS: (*After a momentary hesitation*) Because we have no wish to arouse curiosity in – certain quarters.

FRAZER: Won't my inquiries arouse curiosity?

ROSS: (*Shaking his head*) I don't see why they should. You have a perfectly legitimate

	reason for wanting to find him – he owes you money.
CROMBIE:	(*Smiling*) Which makes you the ideal man from our point of view. Besides, you know Harry. You know his haunts, his habits, his friends – everything about him.
FRAZER:	(*Looking at CROMBIE*) Do I, Mr Crombie? I'm beginning to wonder …
ROSS:	(*Quietly, but rather incisive*) Do you want the job, Mr Frazer – or don't you?
FRAZER:	I certainly want a job – but whether I want this one or not, I'm not sure. You see, I'm the sort of chap who likes to get things straight.
ROSS:	Well?
FRAZER:	I don't know you, and you know very little about me, so …
ROSS:	(*Opens the drawer in his desk and takes out a folder*) On the contrary, we know a great deal about you. Otherwise you wouldn't be sitting in this office. (*Puts the file down on the desk*) There's your dossier.

FRAZER rises and turns the pages in the folder slowly. He looks up.

FRAZER:	Yes, well – er – that's my dossier all right. I wish I knew as much about you, Mr Ross.
ROSS:	During the war I was attached to the Naval Section of M.I.5. In '52 I was asked to form a new department – this department, Mr Frazer. I won't bore you with the broader aspects of our organisation, except to say that we're concerned with security, and for a government department we have at least one unique feature – unlimited funds. (*Smiling*)

	So you won't be underpaid, if that's what you're thinking.
FRAZER:	That's not what I was thinking.
ROSS:	No? I'm delighted to hear it. Well, what's your answer?
FRAZER:	(*After a momentary hesitation*) I'll find Harry Denston for you.
ROSS:	(*Rising*) Good …
FRAZER:	But first of all you must tell me something.
ROSS:	Well?
FRAZER:	Why are you interested in Harry? Why do you want to find him?

ROSS looks across at CROMBIE before replying.

ROSS:	Denston had an appointment with someone in Henton.
FRAZER:	Yes, with me.
ROSS:	No, not primarily with you. You were invited to Henton merely as a cover for Denston's meeting with someone else.
FRAZER:	Well, who was this someone else?
ROSS:	A man called Anstrov.
FRAZER:	Anstrov? You mean the Russian sailor? The chap that died?
ROSS:	Yes. We think that Anstrov was meant to be put ashore at Henton, but the shipwreck upset the plan and the rendezvous didn't come off.
FRAZER:	But why should Harry want to get in touch with Anstrov?
ROSS:	That, I'm afraid, we can't tell you – not at the moment, at any rate. However, find Denston for us, and then we'll tell you.

CROMBIE: We have one clue, Frazer. We think it's an important one. (*Indicates FRAZER's wallet*) It's in your wallet.

FRAZER opens his wallet and looks through it, then takes out the garage ticket.

FRAZER: (*Puzzled*) The garage ticket?

ROSS: (*Nodding*) Yes.

FRAZER: (*To CROMBIE*) So that's why you took the wallet?

CROMBIE: (*Nodding*) Yes. I've checked with the garage. (*Pointing to the ticket*) That's for Denston's car.

FRAZER: Harry's car? (*He looks at CROMBIE*) A Hillman Minx?

CROMBIE: Yes.

FRAZER: … PMR 138.

CROMBIE: That's right. It was left there with the key just over a week ago. It was originally left for one night, then the owner phoned the garage to say it wouldn't be picked up for a week or so. They don't know Denston at the garage, they simply go by the ticket. You've got one half – the other's on the car.

FRAZER: (*Looking at the ticket*) I see. (*He looks at CROMBIE*) And you think that …

CROMBIE: Our theory is that Anstrov had the ticket just in case something went wrong and Harry didn't show up at Henton.

FRAZER: In which case Anstrov would have picked up the car?

ROSS nods.

FRAZER: And the car would have led him to Harry?

ROSS: That's what we think. But we could be wrong, of course.

FRAZER: Well – it certainly explains why Anstrov
                 had this. (*He looks at the ticket*) The
                 Brompton Road Garage … well I've got the
                 ticket, so I suppose I'd better pick up the
                 car.

ROSS nods.

CUT TO: A Garage Reception at Marble Arch. Day.
*FRAZER goes to the reception desk. He gives the ticket to
the man at the desk. He stamps it and gives him the car keys.*

CUT TO: The Workshop of the Garage. Day.
*An Attendant is cleaning a car. FRAZER enters and gives
him the ticket. The man looks at it and then leads the way to
a Hillman Minx. He takes another ticket from the
windscreen-wiper of the car and compares it with the ticket
that FRAZER has given him. FRAZER gets into the car,
starts it, and drives it towards the exit.*

CUT TO: Back Street. Day.
This is a quiet back street in London. The Hillman pulls up
at the kerb.

CUT TO: Inside the Car. Day.
*FRAZER looks around the car. He looks in the map pocket,
takes out the contents, but finds nothing of any interest. He
opens the glove compartment and takes out a duster, a pair
of driving gloves, dark glasses, an A.A. guide and, finally, a
spectacle case. It contains a pair of spectacles. On the lid of
the case there is a label with a name and address on it. It
reads:- "Mrs Ruth Edwards, Talltree Cottage, Cobham."*

CUT TO: Theatre Dressing Room. Day.

HELEN is sitting at her dressing table removing her make-up. The telephone rings.

HELEN: Hello …?

CUT TO: A Telephone Booth. Day.

FRAZER is in the booth. He has the spectacle case in his hands.

FRAZER: Helen?

HELEN: Oh, hello, Tim.

FRAZER: Helen, I'm sorry to disturb you – but do you happen to know a woman called Ruth Edwards?

CUT TO: HELEN's Dressing Room. Day.

HELEN: Ruth Edwards? No, I don't think so, darling. Should I?

CUT TO: The Telephone Booth.

FRAZER: I wondered if she was a friend of Harry's?

HELEN: Well, if she was he kept very quiet about it! Why do you ask?

FRAZER: Well … I found her spectacle case in – All right, thank you, Helen.

CUT TO: HELEN's Dressing Room.

HELEN: No, Tim, wait a minute! I'd like to know if this woman –

CUT TO: The Telephone Booth

FRAZER: I'll explain later. See you soon.

FRAZER hangs up the receiver as does HELEN.

CUT TO: A Country Road. Day.

The Hillman is driving along. It comes to several cottages. In the garden of one of them a GIRL of about ten is playing with a ball. The car passes the cottages, then pulls in to the side of the road and stops. FRAZER gets out and walks slowly back to the cottages.

CUT TO: The Cottages. Day.

The GIRL is playing in the garden. The name of the cottage is on the gate – Talltree Cottage. FRAZER stops at the gate, looks at the name and enters into the garden. He goes to the front door. The GIRL stops playing and comes out to him.

FRAZER: Does Mrs Edwards live here?

The GIRL nods shyly and starts to bounce her ball at her feet and catch it. FRAZER knocks on the front door.

FRAZER: And what's your name?

The GIRL lets her attention wander from the ball to look at FRAZER.

GIRL: (*Shyly*) Anya.

The GIRL walks down the path with her ball. FRAZER stares after her.

End of Episode One

Episode Two

OPEN TO: Outside Talltree Cottage. Day.

FRAZER is standing outside the front door of Talltree Cottage. He is staring after the girl, ANYA, who has run down the garden path after her ball. Still puzzled, he turns to the door and rings the bell. After a few moments the door opens and RUTH EDWARDS stands in the doorway.

RUTH: Yes?

FRAZER: Mrs Edwards?

RUTH: That's right.

RUTH now opens the door fully and we see that she is a good-looking grey-haired woman of about fifty-five. FRAZER takes the spectacles case from his pocket.

FRAZER: I'm sorry to trouble you. Mrs Edwards – but do these happen to be yours?

FRAZER hands the case to RUTH. For a moment she looks at it in bewilderment.

RUTH: Why, yes – they're my spectacles! I'd given them up a long time ago! You found them?

FRAZER: Yes.

RUTH: But where? I made enquiries everywhere ... Oh, I'm so sorry – please come in.

FRAZER: Thank you.

FRAZER steps into the hall.

RUTH: (*Calling*) Anya! Time for tea, dear. Into the kitchen and wash your hands.

RUTH goes into the house, leaving the door open.

CUT TO: The Cottage Sitting Room. Day.

RUTH enters and joins FRAZER.

RUTH: Donald – I've got my spectacles back! (*To FRAZER*) Oh, please take off your coat and sit down.

FRAZER: Well, I ...

RUTH: Please!

33

FRAZER: Very well – thank you.

DONALD EDWARDS enters.

RUTH: Oh, Donald, this is Mr …?

FRAZER: Frazer. Tim Frazer.

RUTH: This is my husband, Mr Frazer.

FRAZER: (*Extending his hand*) How d'you do?

EDWARDS smiles, taking FRAZER's hand.

RUTH: I'm delighted, Donald. Mr Frazer's very kindly brought me my spectacles.

EDWARDS: Spectacles?

RUTH: (*Faintly exasperated*) Yes, you know! The ones I lost three weeks ago – the day I went up to London.

EDWARDS: Oh, yes – of course!

RUTH: (*To FRAZER*) I can't tell you how delighted I am to have them again, Mr Frazer. I've been quite lost without them these last few weeks.

EDWARDS: You've got your new ones, my dear!

RUTH: Oh, yes, I know – but they've never been quite the same; you know that, Donald! (*To FRAZER*) Where on earth did you find them? As far as I could remember I left them in a little restaurant off Regent Street. I telephoned the next day but they said no one had handed them in.

FRAZER looks carefully at RUTH as he answers.

FRAZER: As a matter of fact, I found them in a car.

EDWARDS: In a car?

FRAZER: Yes. It was lent to me by a friend of mine – a man called Harry Denston.

RUTH looks puzzled.

EDWARDS: Harry Denston? (*To RUTH*) I don't think we know anyone of that name, do we, dear?

RUTH: No. No, I don't think so …
EDWARDS: He must have picked them up in the restaurant, or wherever it was you left them.
RUTH: Yes. I suppose he must have done. (*To FRAZER*) Did he ask you to bring them to me, Mr Frazer?
FRAZER: No. I haven't seen Harry; not for some time – not since I borrowed the car, in fact. I came across the glasses quite by chance, and since I was on my way to Amersham, I thought I'd drop them in on you.

ANYA comes in.

RUTH: How very kind! (*To the child*) Anya, look! My spectacles – the ones I lost. This kind gentleman's brought them all the way from London.
EDWARDS: You've gone to a great deal of trouble, Mr Frazer.
FRAZER: Not at all.
RUTH: I can't tell you how grateful I am.
ANYA: Is Mr Frazer staying to tea?
RUTH: (*Laughing*) Yes, dear, I think that's the least we can do. (*To FRAZER*) You will stay and have a cup of tea with us, won't you, Mr Frazer?
FRAZER: (*Looking at his wristwatch*) Well …
RUTH: I just won't take no for an answer!
EDWARDS: That means you're staying, Mr Frazer.

They all laugh.

RUTH: (*To the child*) Come along, Anya, my dear. You can help me in the kitchen.

RUTH and ANYA go out into the kitchen.

FRAZER: What a charming child!

EDWARDS: Yes. We're both devoted to her. I'm afraid we just couldn't bear the thought of parting with her now. (*Suddenly with a little laugh*) Oh, I beg your pardon! You've probably got the wrong idea! She's not our daughter, you know.

FRAZER: Oh, really?

EDWARDS: Oh, no. Ruth and I haven't any children. Anya's my brother-in-law's child. He's a widower, so she spends most of her time with us.

FRAZER: Oh, I see. It's an unusual name – Anya?

EDWARDS: Yes, I suppose it is. I don't quite know how she came by it. I know she used to be teased about it when she first started school.

FRAZER: Yes.

FRAZER crosses to the mantelpiece and looks closely at some model ships that are on it.

FRAZER: (*Pointing to the models*) I say, what wonderful models. Did you make them?

EDWARDS: Yes.

FRAZER: It's beautifully done. It must be a fascinating hobby.

EDWARDS: Yes – only it's rather more than a hobby with me, now, I'm afraid.

FRAZER: (*Turning from the mantelpiece*) Really? You sell them, then?

EDWARDS: Oh dear me, yes! Indeed, yes. There's quite a market for this sort of thing. You'd be surprised. If you'd care to pop into my den for a minute, I could show you some of my other pieces.

FRAZER: Yes, I'd like that.

They go into a small room and cross to the table which contains several models in various stages of construction.

EDWARDS: I've always been fascinated by ships, you know. Naval History – the Age of Sail – that sort of thing.

FRAZER: Were you in the Navy?

EDWARDS: (*Shaking his head; regretfully*) No, unfortunately. It was always my ambition, of course, but – they turned me down. Said my heart was dicky. Ridiculous stuff and nonsense, of course! Sound as a bell! Never had a day's illness in my life! Still – there we are. (*Smiling at FRAZER*) So instead of the real thing, I have to be content with models, Mr Frazer. (*Touching FRAZER's arm*) Mark you, they've got their romance too, you know. Like that for instance.

EDWARDS picks up a model from the table and hands it to FRAZER.

FRAZER: (*Examining the model*) It's beautiful …

EDWARDS: Yes, but I'm a little bit concerned about that one.

FRAZER: Concerned? Why? It looks perfect to me …

EDWARDS: Do you really think so? (*Shaking his head*) Well, it's a funny thing, you know, but I'm not at all sure whether she's genuine or not.

FRAZER: Genuine?

EDWARDS: Oh, I'm sorry, Mr Frazer, it must all sound like Greek to you. Let me explain, all the models I build are reconstructions of actual vessels; ships that really existed.

FRAZER: Oh, I see. You mean, they're scale models.

EDWARDS: Well, no – not exactly scale models, although naturally I try to reconstruct them as accurately as possible. I work mainly from old prints. That one's a frigate called the North Star. (*Points to an illustration in a book*) Here is it, here. You see?

FRAZER: Why, yes.

EDWARDS: There's an interesting story attached to the North Star. (*He looks at FRAZER*) She left Plymouth Harbour one morning in April, 1794. She was only a few miles out into the Channel when a freak storm blew up; one of the worst storms in history. It seemed that nothing could live in such a storm and yet, thanks to the prayers of the local people, and the courage of the rescuers, nearly eight people were saved.

FRAZER: (*After a moment*) It's an interesting story, Mr Edwards. (*Examining the model again*) And a beautiful model. (*He puts it down*)

EDWARDS: Yes. Yes, but I wish I felt happier about it. (*He points to the book*) I've got a nasty feeling that the illustrations may not be genuine – that it's not really the North Star. What do you think, Mr Frazer?

FRAZER looks at EDWARDS for a second, then smiles.

FRAZER: I'm afraid I wouldn't know, sir. I know very little about these things.

EDWARDS: No. No, I suppose not.

ANYA appears in the doorway.

ANYA: Uncle Donald – tea's ready.

EDWARDS: Hm? Oh, yes? Thank you, Anya. Come along, Mr Frazer. I've taken up quite enough of your valuable time.

FRAZER smiles, and they cross towards the sitting room.
The camera slowly pans in on the model of the North Star.

CUT TO: The Mews Outside FRAZER's Flat. Day.
A car draws up outside the front door. It is driven by HELEN BAKER. HELEN gets out of the car.

CUT TO: FRAZER's Drawing Room. Day.
The telephone on the desk is ringing. FRAZER comes out of the bedroom wearing a dressing gown over his trousers. He goes to the desk and picks up the phone. We hear CROMBIE's voice.

FRAZER: Sloane 0181 …
CROMBIE: Frazer?
FRAZER: Speaking.

CUT TO: CROMBIE's Office. Day.
CROMBIE: This is Crombie. I believe you telephoned me.

CUT TO: FRAZER's Drawing Room. Day.
FRAZER: Yes, I did. I tried to get you last night. I've got something to tell you, Crombie.

CUT TO: CROMBIE's Office. Day.
CROMBIE: Is it important?
FRAZER: I think so.
CROMBIE: In that case we'd better meet. It's just after eleven now. Let's say, twelve-thirty – is that all right?

CUT TO: FRAZER's Drawing Room. Day.
FRAZER: Yes, that's fine.
The doorbell rings.
CROMBIE: Good. I'll meet you at my club. Royal Service. St. James's.
FRAZER: I'll be there.

39

FRAZER replaces the receiver and then exits to the hall. We hear the front door open and the sound of voices. HELEN BAKER enters followed by FRAZER.

FRAZER: I thought you were Mrs Glover. I was just going to ask you to clean out the fridge.

HELEN: I'd be delighted if I had a little more time, but I'm on my way to the hairdresser's, and I'm late already.

FRAZER: Oh – well, it's no use asking you to have any coffee then?

HELEN: No, darling. I got your message last night. What do you want to see me about?

FRAZER: (*A moment*) I wondered if you'd do something for me?

HELEN: Yes, of course. What is it?

FRAZER: It may sound rather an odd request, Helen, but I'd like you to make out a list for me …

HELEN: A list of what?

FRAZER: All Harry's friends and acquaintances.

HELEN: (*Surprised*) Harry's friends?

FRAZER: Yes. I probably know quite a lot of them myself, but I daresay there's a few I don't know.

HELEN: Yes. I daresay there is. But what on earth do you want a list of his friends for?

FRAZER: (*After a moment; taking out his cigarette case*) I'm trying to find Harry.

HELEN: Trying to find him? (*Laughing*) Darling, you talk as if he's disappeared! You know Harry! We shall probably have a postcard any day now from Monte Carlo –

FRAZER: Maybe – but supposing we don't?

HELEN: What do you mean?

40

FRAZER:	I can't afford to wait, Helen. I've got to find Harry.
HELEN:	(*Seriously*) But why? You didn't feel like this when you came back from Henton. I thought you'd rather given him up as a bad job.
FRAZER:	Yes, well, I've changed my mind.
HELEN:	Why?
FRAZER:	I've thought better of it, that's all.
HELEN:	Look, Tim, if it's the money that's worrying you – well, you know my feelings about that.
FRAZER:	Yes, I do, Helen, and you can put that right out of your head. You're not paying Harry's debts for him.
HELEN:	Then it is the money!
FRAZER:	All right then, it's the money! (*Crosses to the mantelpiece and picks up the cigarette lighter*) Why the hell should Harry get away with it? Why should someone else always carry the can for him?
HELEN:	(*With a little smile*) No reason at all – but someone always does. Are the firm's creditors making a nuisance of themselves?
FRAZER:	No.
HELEN:	Then why have you changed your mind?
FRAZER:	I've told you, I ...
HELEN:	You haven't told me anything – except that you want to find Harry. Is there another reason – apart from the money?
FRAZER:	No.
HELEN:	Harry isn't in trouble?
FRAZER:	No more than usual.

41

HELEN:	(*Shaking her head*) You know what I mean – serious trouble.
FRAZER:	Why should he be? Besides, if he is, he can take care of himself.
HELEN:	(*Quietly; facing FRAZER*) Tim, as far as Harry's concerned, there's no need to hide anything from me, you know that. I know what he's like, only too well, but I'm in love with him and if he's in some kind of trouble I want to know about it.
FRAZER:	Helen – I've got to find Harry and I've got to find him as quickly as possible. If you can let me have that list – a list of his friends – I'd be very grateful.
HELEN:	And that's all you're going to tell me?
FRAZER:	That's all I can tell you, Helen.
HELEN:	All right. I'll get started on the list straight away and drop it in tomorrow some time, probably after the theatre.
FRAZER:	Thank you. Now what about that coffee – are you sure you won't have a cup?
HELEN:	Yes, I'm quite sure. I must fly.

HELEN looks at FRAZER for a moment, then turns towards the hall.

CUT TO: Inside A London Club. Day.
A WAITER is standing at a sideboard laden with bottles, decanters, glasses etc. He pours two glasses of Sherry and puts them on a silver tray. He turns away from the sideboard with the tray.

CUT TO: The Smoking Room of the London Club. Day.
CROMBIE and FRAZER are sitting in two armchairs beside a low table.

42

CROMBIE:	… and did you find out the name of the little girl? Her surname, I mean?
FRAZER:	No I didn't. Edwards simply said that she was his niece and that she spent most of her time with them.
CROMBIE:	With Donald Edwards and his wife?
FRAZER:	I suppose the name Anya could be a coincidence?
CROMBIE:	It could be.
FRAZER:	But you don't think it is?
CROMBIE:	Well, let's take a look at the facts. Anya was the name mentioned by Anstrov, the Russian sailor – the man that died.
FRAZER:	Yes.
CROMBIE:	Anstrov had some sort of a tie-up with Harry Denston and was supposed to pick up his car. Instead, you picked it up and found a pair of spectacles in it. The spectacles belonged to a woman called Mrs Edwards who, curiously enough, has a neice called Anya. (*Smiling*) Does it really sound like a coincidence, Mr Frazer?
FRAZER:	No. No, I must admit it doesn't, but – I can't help thinking about Donald Edwards and his wife. They're the most harmless looking couple you've ever seen.
CROMBIE:	It's surprising, the number of apparently harmless people who turn up on the front pages of our newspapers. However, let's just run over your description of Donald Edwards again, shall we? See if there's anything we've missed.
FRAZER:	Well, he's about fifty-five. Five foot nine, I should say. Hasn't got much hair. Seems to

	be absent minded – no, not absent minded exactly – abstracted, that's the word. Quite neatly dressed; grey flannel trousers, double-breasted blazer with brass buttons.
CROMBIE:	Regimental buttons?
FRAZER:	No; plain buttons, I particularly noticed that. Well – that's about all. Oh, and I noticed he carried his handkerchief in his cuff – his left cuff.
CROMBIE:	Anything else?
FRAZER:	No. He was very taken up with his models, of course. I told you that.

CROMBIE nods.

FRAZER:	Especially the North Star.
CROMBIE:	(*Non-commitally*) Yes. (*Changing the subject*) Tell me about Mrs Edwards. What's she like?
FRAZER:	About the same age as her husband. Slightly taller, perhaps. Grey hair, short-sighted, I should imagine. Seems to wear the trousers in the family, but one can never really tell. Obviously very fond of the little girl.

CROMBIE nods again and makes no comment. The WAITER arrives with the drinks; he puts the two glasses down on the table and then goes. CROMBIE picks up a glass of Sherry and hands it to FRAZER.

| FRAZER: | (*Taking the glass*) Thank you. |

CROMBIE picks up the other glass of Sherry.

| FRAZER: | I've been in touch with several of Harry's friends since I saw you last, but they've no idea where he is. |
| CROMBIE: | And his fiancée, Miss Baker? |

FRAZER: I saw her this morning. Her feeling is that
            he's on the Riviera, having a holiday. I must
            admit that's his usual form.
CROMBIE: Yes, well he's not on the Riviera this time,
            Mr Frazer. I'm sure of that.

CROMBIE sips his Sherry.

FRAZER: (*After a moment*) Crombie, why do you
            want Harry Denston?
CROMBIE: You asked Ross that question.
FRAZER: Yes, I know, and he didn't give me an
            answer – at least, not a satisfactory one.
CROMBIE: And I'm afraid I can't give you one, either;
            at least not at the moment. (*Looking at
            FRAZER*) And even if I could I'm not sure
            that I would, Frazer. I know this kind of
            work. Take it from me, there are times when
            it's best not to know the whys and the
            wherefores. Just do the job, avoid the
            complications, and don't get involved.
FRAZER: Yes, well, that isn't quite as easy as it
            sounds; not for me at any rate.
CROMBIE: Why not for you?
FRAZER: Because I'm already involved. Harry
            Denston and I were partners, you know that.
            That's why Ross gave me the job in the first
            place.
CROMBIE: Well?
FRAZER: Well, I've got to be in on things, Crombie.
            I've got to know what's going on.
CROMBIE: But you do know what's going on. We're
            trying to find Harry Denston.
FRAZER: That isn't enough. I've got to have more
            than that. I've got to know why I'm looking

	for Harry – and what's going to happen when I find him.
CROMBIE:	Why should you worry about what happens to him – he's no friend of yours?
FRAZER:	Who told you that?
CROMBIE:	Why damn it, man, he owes you over five thousand pounds!
FRAZER:	Yes, that's true – well over five thousand pounds. And he's let me down, Crombie – not once, but half a dozen times. (*Shaking his head*) But he's still a friend of mine; and strange though it may seem I've a very soft spot for Harry Denston.
CROMBIE:	(*Looking at FRAZER*) Why didn't you tell us this before?
FRAZER:	I was annoyed because Harry didn't turn up at Henton. I've cooled off a bit since then.
CROMBIE:	I see. (*He picks up his Sherry and drinks it and looks at FRAZER*)
FRAZER:	Well?

CROMBIE puts down his Sherry.
There is a pause.

CROMBIE:	There's only one thing I can tell you. If you really do like Harry Denston, if you really do have a soft spot for him, then – find him, believe me, Frazer, you'll certainly be doing him a favour. (*He rises*) Now, if you'll excuse me, I have a luncheon appointment.
FRAZER:	(*Also rising*) Crombie, wait a moment.
CROMBIE:	(*Turning*) Well?
FRAZER:	(*After a moment; changing his mind*) It doesn't matter. I've still got Harry's car – the Hillman. What shall I do with it?
CROMBIE:	Have you got a car of your own?

46

FRAZER: No; I sold mine when the firm went broke. (*With the suggestion of a smile*) Harry didn't think it was necessary to part with his.

CROMBIE: Then I should use it. (*He shakes hands with FRAZER*) Let me know if anything turns up.

CROMBIE turns and crosses the room. FRAZER hesitates, then picks up his hat and coat from another chair and starts to put them on as he moves out of frame. The WAITER comes over and starts to clear the glasses and empty the ashtray.

CUT TO: FRAZER's Drawing Room. Day.

The telephone is ringing. FRAZER enters wearing his overcoat and hat and with a folded evening newspaper under his arm. He crosses to the telephone and picks up the receiver.

FRAZER: Hello?

At the other end of the line we hear the voice of EDGAR TUPPER. He has a rather hoarse voice with a slight Cockney accent.

TUPPER: Is that Sloane 0181?

FRAZER: Yes, that's right. Who is it speaking?

TUPPER: I just seen your advert in the paper.

FRAZER: (*Puzzled*) Advert? What advert?

TUPPER: In the evening paper, about your car. Sounds jus' the sort of bus I been looking for.

FRAZER: Look – I'm sorry, I think you must have the wrong number. I haven't advertised any car for sale.

TUPPER: Now, wait a minute! That is Sloane 0181, ain't it?

FRAZER: Yes.

47

TUPPER:	Well – have you, or have you not got a 1956 drophead, Hillman Minx – one owner, 30,000 on the clock?
FRAZER:	(*After a moment's hesitation*) Yes, I have.
TUPPER:	Well – what are you going on about then? Your advert's in the evening paper. Right?
FRAZER:	Wrong.
TUPPER:	Look – I'm a busy man, mister. Get yourself sorted out and call me back, will you? Tupper's the name – Edgar Tupper. Broxbourne 5101.

There is a click from the telephone as TUPPER hangs up. FRAZER slowly replaces the receiver. Obviously puzzled he suddenly picks up his evening paper, opens it, and scans the classified columns. He finds the advertisement he wants. It reads: "Hillman Minx, 1956 Drophead. One owner, Thirty thousand miles. Offers. SLO 0181". FRAZER stares at the advertisement for a moment, then at the telephone; he makes a quick decision. He picks up the receiver and dials a number. We hear the number ringing out and after a little while TUPPER answers the phone.

TUPPER:	Tupper's Garage.
FRAZER:	My name's Frazer. You spoke to me a few minutes ago about the advert in the evening paper.
TUPPER:	Oh, yes. You've remembered it now, have you?
FRAZER:	Are you interested in the car, Mr …?
TUPPER:	Tupper. Well, I wasn't phoning about your health! Bring it round and let's have a dekko at it.
FRAZER:	Where are you?
TUPPER:	On the Cambridge Road just past Wormley. Turn right at the traffic lights – it's about a

mile down Station Lane. Tupper's Garage – you can't miss it.

FRAZER: What time would suit you?

TUPPER: Any time, chum. I'm here all day. All the ruddy day. You can't miss it. Tupper's Garage.

FRAZER: All right – I'll be there in about an hour. (*He rings off and replaces the receiver*)

CUT TO: TUPPER's Garage.

This is a slightly down-at-heel filling station with a small sales yard attached to it.

EDGAR TUPPER is filling a CUSTOMER's car from one of the pumps. He finishes with the pump, hangs it up, and comes to the driver's window, obsequiously touching his hat.

TUPPER: (To the DRIVER) That'll be a pound, exactly, if you please, Mr Wentworth.

DRIVER: (*Grinning*) Okay, Tupper (*Handing TUPPER a pound note*) Keep the change.

The DRIVER drives off. TUPPER looks at the note in disgust, spits after the car, and puts the note in his pocket. FRAZER's (HARRY DENSTON's) Hillman drives up and pulls in behind the pumps. FRAZER gets out and walks across to TUPPER who is still staring after the other car. As FRAZER comes up beside him he jerks a thumb in the direction in which the car has gone. He still doesn't look round at FRAZER.

TUPPER: Bloody skinflint! Throws his money about like a man with no arms.

FRAZER: Mr Tupper? My name's Frazer. I telephoned you about the Hillman.

TUPPER: I see the Hillman come in, I thought it'd be you.

FRAZER: Well – do you want to have a look at it?

TUPPER turns and looks at FRAZER rather blankly.

TUPPER: Yes. Might as well, I suppose.

Together they walk over to the Hillman. While FRAZER watches him TUPPER slowly walks round the car, examining the body. He gets in the driver's seat and starts the engine. He listens to it running for a moment, then gets out of the car, opens the bonnet, and pokes around inside. He closes the bonnet again and stops the engine.

TUPPER: Not bad; seen worse.

TUPPER walks away into the office. FRAZER follows him.

CUT TO: TUPPER's Office. Day.

TUPPER enters followed by FRAZER.

TUPPER: What do you want for it, then?

FRAZER: Oh, I don't know. What do you think?

TUPPER: Cor stone us! You're a right one, you are! First of all you forget all about your advert – then you don't even know how much you want for it. Do you want a drop? No thank you.

FRAZER: Well, I hadn't given it a lot of thought. I only decided to sell it on the spur of the moment.

TUPPER: Well, if you've got no price in mind, I'll make you an offer. Five hundred quid.

FRAZER: (*Musing*) Five hundred …

TUPPER: It's a good price for that year, you know. You won't get no higher anywhere else.

FRAZER: Oh, I don't know …

TUPPER: You won't, you know.

FRAZER: Five hundred – is that the highest you'll go?

TUPPER: Well, I didn't say that, did I? I mean, you just said you hadn't given it much thought,

	so I give you a price. (*Smiling*) I'm not in this business for the fun of it.
FRAZER:	I'm sorry. Five hundred doesn't interest me.
TUPPER:	It doesn't? Then you must have some idea what you want for it. Give me a figure.
FRAZER:	I'll tell you what, Mr Tupper, you make me another offer, Mr Tupper.

TUPPER considers this for a moment.

TUPPER:	All right. Five-seven-five. And that's it – the top.
FRAZER:	Five-seven-five? That's quite a jump.
TUPPER:	Yes, well, it's in pretty fair nick really, I suppose. Tyres and everything. It's not a bad motor – I don't want to do you do I?
FRAZER:	(*Looking at the car, then at TUPPER; after a moment*) No – I think I can do better than that.
TUPPER:	(*Annoyed*) Not with Edgar Tupper, you can't.
FRAZER:	(*Turning away*) All right.
TUPPER:	(*Suddenly; stopping FRAZER*) No, wait a minute!

FRAZER stops; turns.

TUPPER:	I've offered you five hundred and seventy-five, now that's a very fair offer. What more do you want?
FRAZER:	(*Calmly*) I want a hundred pounds more.
TUPPER:	You – what?
FRAZER:	You heard me. I want a hundred pounds more.
TUPPER:	Six hundred and seventy-five quid?
FRAZER:	(*Nodding*) That's right.
TUPPER:	Why, you're up the wall man! That car isn't worth six hundred and seventy-five.

FRAZER:	I never said it was – I said that's what I wanted for it.
TUPPER:	(*Irritated and not quite so sure of himself*) I'll give you six hundred.
FRAZER:	(*Shaking his head*) No, Mr Tupper. The price is six hundred and seventy-five.
TUPPER:	(*Stopping him*) Look, I'll tell you what I'll do. I want to be fair about this. I don't want to be difficult. I'll give you six hundred and twenty …
FRAZER:	(*Interrupting him*) You'll give me nothing of the sort. If you want that car, you'll pay what I'm asking for it.
TUPPER:	But it's not worth anything like six hundred and seventy-five. Why, blimey, I can get a new one for just over eight hundred!
FRAZER:	Yes, but you don't want a new one, do you?
TUPPER:	What do you mean?
FRAZER:	I mean that, unless I'm very much mistaken, you want that car. That particular car.
TUPPER:	Well – I don't know about that particular car; I certainly want one like it.
FRAZER:	Why?
TUPPER:	(*Looking at FRAZER*) I've got a customer waiting for it – that's why.
FRAZER:	Why doesn't he buy a new one?
TUPPER:	Don't ask me why he doesn't buy a new one! Gawd knows! Must be like this, he says. Drophead – same colour – same year – same mileage; the lot.
FRAZER:	Well, there you are. Six hundred and seventy-five …
TUPPER:	It's crazy. It's just ruddy ridiculous!
FRAZER:	Who is this customer of yours?

TUPPER: Don't be daft, do you think I'm going to tell you that – so you can go behind my back and do a deal with him? Come off it chum!

FRAZER: Well, to prove my point, I'll tell you what I'll do. You tell me who this customer of yours is, and you can have the car for six hundred.

TUPPER: (*Looking at FRAZER; curious*) There's a catch somewhere.

FRAZER: There's no catch.

TUPPER: No?

FRAZER: No.

TUPPER: (*After a moment's consideration*) Well, I'll tell you what I'll do.

FRAZER: Yes?

TUPPER: (*Smiling*) I'll give you what you're asking. Six-seven-five.

FRAZER: (*A moment*) All right, it's a deal.

TUPPER: Okay.

FRAZER: But won't your client want to see the car? I mean …

TUPPER: No, no, don't worry about that. He trusts me, my client does. He knows what he's getting. You just leave her here and I'll make out the cheque.

FRAZER: No, Mr Tupper. No cheques, if you don't mind – cash.

TUPPER: Cash? You don't think I'm going to have nearly seven hundred quid lying about here in cash, do you?

FRAZER: Well, in that case, I'll bring the car down tomorrow morning. That'll give you time to get the money.

TUPPER: Here – I'll tell you what. If you leave it here now, I could lend you my car for tonight, and tomorrow morning …

FRAZER: (*Shaking his head*) No. No, thank you. You get the money by tomorrow morning, and I'll bring the Hillman down. I'll be here, Mr Tupper, don't worry. Nine o'clock.

TUPPER: (*Hesitating*) All right. I'll see you then.

FRAZER: Don't forget the cash.

TUPPER nods and FRAZER exits. TUPPER walks to a table and picks up a cup and drinks. We hear Frazer start the engine of the Hillman and drive away.

CUT TO: A Country Lane. Day.

A telephone booth stands on the grass verge.

The Hillman Minx comes into view and pulls up by the side of the telephone box. FRAZER jumps out of the car and goes into the telephone booth.

CUT TO: CROMBIE's Office. Day.

CROMBIE is sitting behind his desk. He picks up the phone.

CROMBIE: Hello?

FRAZER: Is that you, Crombie?

CROMBIE: Yes.

CUT TO: The Phone Box.

FRAZER: This is Frazer. Listen, I think I'm on to something. I've just been offered nearly seven hundred pounds for Harry's car.

CUT TO: CROMBIE's Office.

CROMBIE: Seven hundred? What's it worth?

CUT TO:	The Phone Box.
FRAZER:	Oh – about five-fifty? Six hundred at the outside.
CROMBIE:	Who made the offer?
FRAZER:	A man called Tupper; but he's just the go-between, he's buying it for someone else.
CUT TO:	CROMBIE's Office.
CROMBIE:	How do you know he's the go-between?
FRAZER:	He'd never have offered me that price if he wasn't!
CROMBIE:	I see. How did Tupper get in touch with you in the first place?
CUT TO:	The Phone Box.
FRAZER:	Someone put an advertisement in the evening paper; it described Harry's car and it had my phone number. Look, I'm on my way back to town – can we meet? I'll give you the full details then.
CUT TO:	CROMBIE's Office.
CROMBIE:	Yes, all right. This Mr Tupper sounds interesting. I'll call at your flat in about an hour.
FRAZER:	Right! I'll give you the address. It's –
CROMBIE:	I've got the address, Frazer. I'll see you in an hour.
CUT TO:	The Mews in Kensington.

The Hillman Minx drives into the mews; FRAZER gets out and walks towards the house.

CUT TO: The Hall of FRAZER's Flat. Day.

FRAZER enters the front door. CROMBIE is standing, facing the door. As he sees FRAZER enter, he lifts his arm as if trying to attract attention.

FRAZER: Crombie!

FRAZER reaches CROMBIE who clutches at FRAZER's arm.

FRAZER: Crombie, what is it?

CROMBIE: Frazer … listen … the North Star …

FRAZER: What about the North Star?

CROMBIE: I … want … you … to …

CROMBIE slumps forward into FRAZER's arms. We see a knife stuck in his back. FRAZER stands still – obviously frightened – and as CROMBIE slides to the floor FRAZER rushes towards the drawing room.

CUT TO: The Drawing Room. Day.

FRAZER rushes in and dials 999. He stands holding the telephone – suddenly his eye catches sight of something on the mantelpiece. He lowers the receiver in amazement and goes over to the mantelpiece where the model of the North Star is sitting.

End of Episode Two

Episode Three

OPEN TO: FRAZER's Drawing Room. Day.

FRAZER is staring at the model of the North Star on the mantelpiece. The telephone receiver hangs idly in his hands. On an impulse, he replaces the receiver and goes back into the hall. We see the body of CROMBIE on the floor, the knife protruding from his back. FRAZER stands looking at the body for a moment and then he makes a quick decision. He goes past the body to the front door, opens it, and goes out, closing the door behind him. The camera tracks in to CROMBIE's body.

CUT TO: The Library at 29 Smith Square, London. Day.

Ross is at his desk, writing. There is a knock on the door.

ROSS: Come in!

HOBSON enters.

HOBSON: Mr Frazer wants to see you, sir. He says it's very important.

ROSS: (*Surprised*) Frazer?

FRAZER comes in through the door, pushing past HOBSON.

ROSS: (*Quietly; annoyed*) Thank you, Hobson.

HOBSON goes out, closing the door after him.

ROSS: What is it? I told you to phone Crombie if anything important …

FRAZER: (*Interrupting; tensely*) Crombie's dead!

ROSS stares at FRAZER without speaking, then he moves round his desk to where FRAZER is standing.

ROSS: (*Quietly*) What happened?

FRAZER hesitates, trying to regain his breath.

ROSS: Quickly – tell me …

FRAZER: I arranged to meet Crombie at my flat. When I arrived he was already there. He was in the hall … There was a knife in his back.

ROSS: Have you informed the police?
FRAZER: Not yet. I thought I'd better see you first.
ROSS: (*Nodding*) Good! Have you got your car here?
FRAZER: Yes.
ROSS: Right! (*Crosses to the door*) Tell me the rest of the story in the car.

ROSS opens the door and they go out.

CUT TO: Outside Smith Square. London. Day.
FRAZER and ROSS come out of the front door of the house and get into the Hillman Minx. The car pulls away.

CUT TO: The Hall of FRAZER's Flat. Day.
FRAZER and ROSS enter. FRAZER stops dead – amazed. The body of CROMBIE is no longer there. FRAZER stands transfixed for a moment, then dashes into the drawing room.

CUT TO: FRAZER's Drawing Room. Day.
FRAZER has just come into the room and he dashes to the mantelpiece – the model of the North Star is not there. FRAZER looks wildly round the room as ROSS comes in from the hall.

FRAZER: It's gone! The model's gone!
ROSS: So I see.
FRAZER: But it was there! I swear to you! The model was on the mantelpiece!
ROSS: Frazer, are you sure – quite sure – that Crombie was dead?
FRAZER: Yes, I'm quite sure. (*Facing ROSS*) Ross, I'm telling you the truth! They were both here twenty minutes ago! Crombie was lying in the hall and the model was on the mantelpiece!

60

ROSS looks at FRAZER.

FRAZER: It's the truth – don't you believe me?

ROSS: (*Quietly*) Let's get this sorted out. Sit down, Frazer.

FRAZER hesitates, then sits on the arm of the chair.

ROSS: Just after lunch you had a phone call from this man – what was his name – Tupper?

FRAZER nods.

ROSS: You say that Tupper wanted to buy the car from you – Harry Denston's car?

FRAZER: That's right. He said he'd seen it advertised in the evening paper.

ROSS: Did you put the advertisement in the paper?

FRAZER: No, but someone did – I saw it.

ROSS: Did Tupper give any reason for wanting the car?

FRAZER: He did later, when I saw him. He said it was for a customer.

ROSS: (*Nodding*) So you saw Tupper, did the deal, and arranged to deliver the car tomorrow morning?

FRAZER: Yes; although eventually he tried to talk me into leaving the car with him this afternoon.

ROSS: Why didn't you leave it?

FRAZER: Well – for two reasons. I wanted to get Crombie's reaction to the Tupper incident, and I wanted another opportunity to go over the car again – just in case I'd missed something.

ROSS: How did this man, Tupper, strike you.

FRAZER: Oh, bit of a rough diamond, I suppose. But I was more surprised by the price he offered me than anything else. Six hundred and

	seventy-five pounds. The car's not worth that; nothing like it.
ROSS:	What about the garage?
FRAZER:	It looked genuine enough.
ROSS:	I see. Go on. You phoned Crombie …?
FRAZER:	Yes, I phoned him as soon as I got away from Tupper. I told him briefly what had happened and he said he'd meet me here as soon as I got back to Town. Anyway, when I arrived …
ROSS:	How long did it take you?
FRAZER:	From the time I phoned Crombie? About an hour.
ROSS:	Go on.
FRAZER:	Well – when I arrived he was standing in the hall out there. At first I didn't realise anything was wrong. I went up to him and he said something like: "Frazer … the North Star …" Then he fell forward into my arms and I saw the knife in his back.
ROSS:	And then?
FRAZER:	That's about all. I came in here, and dialled 999. Just as I was dialling, I noticed the model of the North Star on the mantelpiece, so I put down the telephone and …
ROSS:	You came to see me?
FRAZER:	Yes.
ROSS:	I see.
FRAZER:	It all sounds pretty improbable now, I'm afraid; but I assure you …
ROSS:	Don't worry, I'm used to improbable stories and, actually, this particular one isn't at all improbable. Crombie's body may have gone – but there's blood on the carpet outside.

(*He looks at FRAZER*) You disturbed them. They were in the flat when you got here.

FRAZER: Who was in the flat?

ROSS ignores the question and crosses to the telephone. He picks up the receiver and dials a number. He stands looking at FRAZER as the number rings out. After a moment we hear the voice of JULIAN HURST on the other end of the line. We do not see HURST.

HURST: Hello? Mayfair 1284 …

ROSS: Hurst? This is Ross …

HURST: Oh, good evening, sir.

ROSS: Hurst, listen. I want you to get on to the Special Branch. Ask for Laidman.

HURST: Yes, sir.

ROSS: Tell him Crombie's dead and ask him to phone me back in the next half hour. (*He looks at the telephone*) Sloane 7211 …

HURST: Yes, sir. (*After a moment*) I'm sorry about Crombie. What happened?

ROSS: (*Ignoring the question*) You've got the number?

HURST: Yes, sir. Sloane 7211 …

ROSS puts down the telephone and turns towards FRAZER who is now mixing himself a drink.

ROSS: May I have one of those?

FRAZER: Yes of course – I'm sorry. Scotch?

ROSS: That'll do nicely. Very little soda.

FRAZER mixes the drink, his hand shaking slightly. ROSS stands watching him.

FRAZER: The first time I saw Crombic hc was ordering a Scotch. It was in the bar at Henton.

63

ROSS: He was one of my best men – and a friend.
               You don't make many friends in this
               business. Arthur Crombie was one of them.

FRAZER says nothing, he turns and brings the drink to
ROSS.

ROSS: How does this affect you?

FRAZER: What do you mean?

ROSS: You don't have to go on with this job if you
               don't want to, you know. We only asked
               you to help us because you know Harry
               Denston, know him well. You're not one of
               us, you can drop out any time you feel like
               it.

FRAZER: I don't feel like it.

ROSS: Aren't you frightened?

FRAZER: Oh yes, I'm frightened – I'm as frightened
               as hell.

ROSS: (*Smiling*) Good. I'm delighted to hear it,
               because you're no good to me unless you're
               frightened, Mr Frazer.

FRAZER: Then I'm your man. (*He holds out his hand;*
               it is still trembling slightly) Isn't there a cure
               for this sort of thing?

ROSS: If there is, I don't recommend it.

FRAZER: Of course, it might help a little if you satisfy
               my curiosity.

ROSS: About Denston?

FRAZER: Yes.

ROSS looks at FRAZER; drinks, then puts his glass down on
the table.

ROSS: Three months ago something was stolen
               from a house in Westminster. We believe
               that this – (*He hesitates*) – particular thing
               passed into the hands of Harry Denston and

	that he intended to hand it over to Anstrov. You know what happened: the plan misfired.
FRAZER:	Which means that Harry's still got the thing you're looking for?
ROSS:	Well – we hope so. It's our job to find him before he gets rid of it.
FRAZER:	I suppose it's no use asking you what it is?
ROSS:	(*Shaking his head*) I've already told you a great deal more than I should have done. Find Harry Denston for us and I'll tell you the rest.
FRAZER:	(*Looking at his glass*) Ross, there's just one point. It's worrying me a little bit because, well – (*Looks at ROSS*)
ROSS:	Go on.
FRAZER:	Do you think Harry Denston murdered Crombie?
ROSS:	Your guess is as good as mine. It might even be better. You know Denston.
FRAZER:	(*Shaking his head*) I don't think he did.
ROSS:	Well, I hope you're right. (*Picks up his drink*) You know, your garage friend interests me just at the moment.
FRAZER:	Tupper?
ROSS:	Yes. Did you say you'd sold him the car?
FRAZER:	Well, yes – I'm supposed to have sold it. He's expecting me to deliver it tomorrow morning.
ROSS:	We'll go over it tonight with a fine tooth-comb. If we don't find anything you can go ahead and keep the appointment.
FRAZER:	Right.

CUT TO: Outside TUPPER's Garage. Next morning.

A large army lorry has broken down and is parked in the road opposite the garage. An ARMY PRIVATE is sitting on the running board smoking a cigarette. An ARMY CORPORAL is walking over to the office where TUPPER sits on a high stool, looking out of the window. The CORPORAL goes into the office. The CORPORAL's name is CAXTON. He is a tall, burly man of about forty.

CUT TO: TUPPER's Office. Day.

CAXTON: You got a heavier tyre-lever than this one mate?

TUPPER: What's the matter with that one, then?

CAXTON: About as much good as a knife and fork on the tyres I got.

TUPPER gets up and rummages in a toolbox on the floor.

TUPPER: Talk about Fred Karno's army! Ain't you got no tools of your own? You've had me jack already!

CAXTON: Don't blame me, mate – I'm only on this thing for a ride. The driver they've given me's dead useless. He's just sitting on his bottom.

TUPPER: (*Handing over a set of tyre-levers*) Why ain't you got a spare?

CAXTON: He left it in the depot.

TUPPER: Cor stone me!

CUT TO: Outside TUPPER's Garage. Day.

The CORPORAL walks back towards the lorry. As he does so the Hillman Minx draws up by the office and FRAZER gets out. He goes into the office.

CUT TO: TUPPER's Office. Day.

TUPPER: Ah, there we are, Mr Frazer. I thought you wasn't coming!

FRAZER: Yes, I know I'm late. I'm sorry. I got held up. Well – there's the car, here's the logbook. (*He produces the book*) Have you got the cash?

TUPPER: I have mate. It's all ready for you.

CAXTON appears again.

CAXTON: All right if I use your phone, cock?

TUPPER: (*Annoyed*) That again? You on to your girlfriend or something?

CAXTON: (*Going towards the phone*) Oh, sure. Trunk call to Hollywood – Brigitte Bardot.

CAXTON crosses to the telephone and dials.

TUPPER: Fred Karno's bloody army! Think they know it all! You going back to London after this?

FRAZER: Yes.

TUPPER: I'll run you to the station.

TUPPER goes to a small safe in the corner and starts to open it.

CAXTON: (*On the phone*) George, this is Bill … Put the Sarge on … Sarge. We're in a mess … A breakdown … No, this is a proper one, Sarge. We can't … He's come out with no tools, no spares – nothing! I know we're late! What am I supposed to do about it? … Yes – they call it a garage! (*Looking at TUPPER*) No – he doesn't know his arse from his elbow!

CAXTON goes on talking in the background as TUPPER gets the safe open and takes out a thick bundle of notes. CAXTON sees the notes and raises his eyes to Heaven.

CAXTON: (*Still on the phone*) I don't know about running a garage, but there's some sort of racket going on here!

TUPPER gives CAXTON a dirty look and hands the money to FRAZER, who puts it into a small attaché case he has with him.

TUPPER: Six hundred and seventy-five … It's all there. You can count it on the way to the station.

FRAZER nods and he and TUPPER leave the office.

CUT TO: Outside TUPPER's Office. Day.

TUPPER and FRAZER come out of the office. TUPPER gets into the driver's seat of the Hillman, FRAZER gets into the passenger seat and the car drives away. CAXTON comes out of the office and watches them.

CUT TO: The Library in Smith Square. Night.

The curtains are drawn and there is a screen on the wall at one end of the room and a film projector on ROSS's desk. A MAN is standing by the projector threading the film into it. ROSS is standing by the desk.

ROSS: All ready?

PROJECTIONIST: Yes, sir.

ROSS looks at his watch. There is a knock on the door.

ROSS: Come in!

The door opens and HOBSON shows FRAZER in. HOBSON goes out again.

ROSS: Hello, Frazer.

FRAZER: I'm sorry if I'm late, sir.

ROSS: That's all right. We've got a film here. I want you to take a look at it. It's Tupper's Garage. We wanted to know what happened after you left.

FRAZER: What did happen?

ROSS: We'll show you the film we took and you can see for yourself. I want you to tell me if you recognise anyone. (*He turns to the PROJECTIONIST*) Ready to go?

PROJECTIONIST: Ready.

The PROJECTIONIST goes to a wall and turns off the light. Then he starts the projector and we see the silent, rather bad quality, film.

CUT TO: The Film taken outside TUPPER's Garage. *We are looking at the garage from the opposite side of the road. TUPPER is outside his office, talking to CAXTON. TUPPER seems rather annoyed. He jerks his head to the office and CAXTON goes in. TUPPER stands outside, looking up and down the road. CAXTON comes out again with a large monkey-wrench. He walks towards the camera and out of vision.*

ROSS's VOICE: This was all taken from inside the lorry, of course.

A Ford Consul, a private hire car, drives up to the pumps and TUPPER immediately crosses to it and shakes hands with the passenger as he gets out of the car. The Ford drives away again and TUPPER leads the visitor to the Hillman Minx. They both stand talking and looking at the car. The visitor wears a trilby and a belted overcoat.

ROSS's VOICE: This is the important bit. Take a good look and tell us whether you've ever seen this man before.

On the film a telescopic lens comes into play and we seem to zoom in on the two men by the Hillman Minx. The man with TUPPER is CAPTAIN NIKIYAN.

FRAZER's VOICE: Good God! That's Nikiyan – the sea captain!

69

NIKIYAN shakes hands with TUPPER, gets into the Hillman Minx and drives it away. The film ends.

CUT TO: The Library in Smith Square. Night.
The lights go up in the room and the PROJECTIONIST starts to re-wind the film.

ROSS: You're certain? You're quite certain that was Captain Nikiyan?

FRAZER: I'm quite certain. There's no doubt at all.

ROSS: Did this man ever see Crombie?

FRAZER: (*After thinking*) Yes – as a matter of fact, he did. When we handed Anstrov's things over to Nikiyan, Crombie was there. I remember Nikiyan shook hands with him.

ROSS: Why?

FRAZER: (*A shrug*) He shook hands with everybody.

ROSS: (*Seriously*) I see.

CAXTON enters. He is now wearing a dark suit. FRAZER stares at him.

CAXTON: (*To FRAZER: with a faint smile*) Hello …

ROSS: Oh – this is Caxton. You saw him at the garage …

FRAZER: Yes, of course! The Corporal!

CAXTON: That's right, cock. (*To ROSS*) Was the film all right, sir?

ROSS: Yes. (*He takes out his cigarette case*)

FRAZER: Look, why did Nikiyan want the Hillman?

ROSS: Presumably because it belonged to Harry Denston.

FRAZER: Yes, but why? Your men went over that car last night from top to bottom. There's nothing unusual about it?

CAXTON: I'll bet Mr Tupper doesn't think so.

FRAZER: What do you mean?

CAXTON: He paid you nearly seven hundred for it –
            right?

FRAZER nods.

CAXTON: And what's it worth?

FRAZER: Oh, five-fifty. Six hundred, perhaps – at the
            outside.

CAXTON: Exactly. And what do you think Nikiyan
            paid?

FRAZER: I don't know.

CAXTON: Neither do I; but knowing your friend,
            Tupper, you can bet your bottom dollar it
            was well over seven hundred. (*To ROSS*)
            There must be something unusual about that
            car, sir.

ROSS: Well, if there is, Caxton, we didn't find it.
            (*He lights his cigarette*)

CUT TO: The Front door of FRAZER's Flat. Night.

*HELEN BAKER comes into view carrying a small valise.
She rings the doorbell. There is a pause, then she rings the
bell again. After a moment the door is opened by FRAZER;
he is wearing a dressing gown.*

CUT TO: The Hall of FRAZER's flat. Night.

FRAZER: Helen, I'm awfully sorry – I was in the
            kitchen.

HELEN enters the flat.

CUT TO: The Drawing room of FRAZER's Flat.
            Night.

HELEN enters, followed by FRAZER.

FRAZER: (*Indicating the tray on the drinks table*) I've
            just made myself some cocoa – would you
            like some?

HELEN:	(*Laughing; horrified*) No, thank you, darling.
FRAZER:	Would you like a drink?
HELEN:	Well, I should certainly prefer it to a cup of cocoa!

FRAZER crosses to the drinks table.

FRAZER:	What would you like?
HELEN:	Oh, anything, sweetie. Have you a gin and tonic?
FRAZER:	Yes, of course.

FRAZER mixes the drink. HELEN puts down the valise and sits on the settee.

HELEN:	My, what a day!
FRAZER:	You sound tired, Helen.
HELEN:	I am. We had a matinee this afternoon.
FRAZER:	(*Bringing the drink to HELEN*) Really?
HELEN:	(*Taking the drink*) A charity thing. They say Charity Begins at Home – and my God, how right they are! There was a wretched woman on the front row with a tea tray. Well, really! I'll swear she balanced it on her head!

FRAZER laughs; returns and picks up the cup of cocoa from the tray. HELEN drinks, then puts down the glass and opens her handbag.

HELEN:	I've made out that list for you, Tim. You know – Harry's friends and acquaintances.
FRAZER:	(*Taking the sheet of notepaper from HELEN*) Oh, thank you, Helen. (*Looking at the list*) I say, you've really gone to town!
HELEN:	Well, you said you wanted me to put down everybody I could think of.
FRAZER:	Yes. Thank you very much. (*Looking at the list*) Who on earth is Mrs Lightweight?

HELEN:	She's the 'daily'. You've seen her. Harry's always going mad about her – she breaks everything.
FRAZER:	(*Laughing*) Yes, of course. (*He folds the paper and puts it in his pocket*)
HELEN:	Tim, why did you want that list?
TIM:	(*Sitting on the arm of the settee*) You know why. I'm trying to find Harry. (*Looking at HELEN*) And I've got to find him, Helen – it's more necessary now than ever.
HELEN:	Yes, but why? (*She rises*) Is Harry in trouble?
FRAZER:	Harry's always in trouble. You know that.
HELEN:	No, I'm serious, Tim. I mean real trouble?
FRAZER:	(*After a moment*) Yes.
HELEN:	Are the police after him?
FRAZER:	No, Helen. It isn't the police.
HELEN:	Then who is it?

FRAZER looks at the cup of cocoa he is holding; he doesn't reply.

HELEN:	And what did you mean when you said: "I've got to find him – it's more necessary now than ever?" Why now?
FRAZER:	I meant that … (*Looking up at HELEN*) Well, someone else was looking for Harry and he … (*Glances in the direction of the hall; remembering CROMBIE*)
HELEN:	Yes?
FRAZER:	He was murdered.
HELEN:	Murdered!
FRAZER:	Yes.
HELEN:	But – do the police know about this murder?
FRAZER:	(*Rising; crossing and putting his drink down on the tray*) Yes, they know about it.

HELEN:	Tim, who was this person? What happened? Tell me …
FRAZER:	(*Turning*) He was a friend of mine. He was helping me to look for Harry and someone stuck a knife in his back. It was as simple as that, Helen.
HELEN:	(*Nervously; with a little laugh*) I don't believe you! You're joking?
FRAZER:	No, I'm not joking.
HELEN:	But – when did this happen?
FRAZER:	Last night.
HELEN:	It isn't in the papers …
FRAZER:	No, I know it isn't. I don't think it will be either. (*He moves towards HELEN*) Helen, please don't think I'm being difficult, but …

FRAZER stops; staring at the briefcase which HELEN has put down near the settee. HELEN follows his gaze. FRAZER crosses and picks up the case.

FRAZER:	Is this yours?
HELEN:	Yes, I brought it – but it's not mine.
FRAZER:	(*Looking at the valise*) Haven't I seen this before somewhere?
HELEN:	Yes, it's possible. It's Harry's.
FRAZER:	Harry's?
HELEN:	Yes.
FRAZER:	Well – why did you bring it here?
HELEN:	I went down to the cottage yesterday and found it in one of the cupboards. I was rather curious about it because …
FRAZER:	What cottage? I didn't know you had a cottage, Helen?
HELEN:	Yes; it's in Surrey, about two miles from Alton. We've had it about six months now.
FRAZER:	We?

74

HELEN:	Harry and I. We used to go down for the odd weekend.
FRAZER:	But good heavens, Helen, why on earth didn't you tell me about it?
HELEN:	I wanted to but Harry wouldn't hear of it. He said it was our secret retreat and he didn't want anyone to know about it.
FRAZER:	I shouldn't have thought I came under the heading of anybody.
HELEN:	Darling, I know, I feel awful about it. But Harry was adamant. (*With a little laugh*) He was terribly secretive and coy about the whole business.
FRAZER:	(*Indicating the briefcase*) You say this was in one of the cupboards.
HELEN:	Yes … After you asked me for that list I wondered if there was any other way I could help you to find him. I knew that Harry had left a few clothes and things at the cottage so I drove down there.
FRAZER:	(*Examining the valise*) Have you opened it?
HELEN:	No, I can't – it's locked. You can try if you like.

FRAZER puts the case down on the arm of the settee and examines the lock.

FRAZER:	Well – it's a pretty good lock, but I could probably force it. I'll get something from the kitchen.

FRAZER goes off into the kitchen. HELEN finishes her drink, then crosses to the settee and looks at the case. FRAZER returns with a small screwdriver.

FRAZER:	This ought to do it.

He puts the screwdriver under the lock of the valise and starts to force it.

FRAZER:	Did Harry ever take any business papers to the cottage?
HELEN:	Harry? He wasn't fond of work at the best of times. No – that's why I was rather intrigued when I found it. I don't really think I've seen it before.
FRAZER:	(*Forcing the case open*) Ah – that's it.

FRAZER opens the briefcase and takes out what appears to be a framed picture.

HELEN:	(*Curious*) What is it – a picture?
FRAZER:	(*After a moment; still looking at the picture*) It's a print – a lithograph.
HELEN:	What an extraordinary thing to keep in a briefcase.

HELEN takes the picture out of FRAZER's hand and looks at it. It is a picture of a sailing ship, a frigate, leaving Portsmouth harbour. There is an inscription on the bottom of the print which reads: The North Star 1794.

CUT TO:	DONALD EDWARDS' Study at Tall Tree Cottage. Night.

Edwards is standing by the desk in his study, looking at the print. He picks up a large magnifying glass and examines the illustration of the North Star. After a moment he puts down the print and magnifying glass and looks across the desk where FRAZER is standing on the other side watching him.

EDWARDS:	… I'm awfully pleased about this. It's taken a great weight off my mind.
FRAZER:	Oh, good! I'm glad.
EDWARDS:	It really is most kind of you to go to all this trouble.
FRAZER:	(*Indicating the print*) I take it, that confirms what you thought then?

EDWARDS: (*Smiling*) It confirms what I'd hoped, Mr Frazer – which is even better!

EDWARDS taps the large book which is on the desk. It is the book we saw in the first scene with DONALD EDWARDS.

EDWARDS: Although the engraving is a different one, the ship is certainly the same – so it seems that the original picture <u>was</u> the North Star after all.

FRAZER: Yes, it's hardly likely that two authors would make the same mistake.

EDWARDS: Quite.

EDWARDS returns to the desk and compares the book with the model of the North Star which is also on the desk.

EDWARDS: One of the things that struck me as odd in the first illustration was the angle of the bow-sprit. I thought it was rather steep for a frigate of that period, but this new engraving quite confirms it.

FRAZER: Yes, so I see.

RUTH EDWARDS comes in from the other room with a cup of tea in each hand. She smiles indulgently at the two men over the model.

RUTH: I thought I'd better bring you a cup of tea, Mr Frazer. I know Donald, once he starts talking about his models.

FRAZER: (*Laughing*) That's very kind of you.

RUTH puts the tea on the desk. EDWARDS straightens up and picks up his cup.

EDWARDS: Thank you, my dear.

RUTH: (*To FRAZER*) But what a coincidence, Mr Frazer – you finding the print, I mean! And so soon after talking with Donald.

FRAZER:	Yes, it's quite extraordinary. But it doesn't belong to me, you know. It belongs to a man called Harry Denston.
RUTH:	Denston? (*To her husband*) That name seems familiar, Donald?
EDWARDS:	I don't think so, my dear.
RUTH:	(*Suddenly to FRAZER*) But of course! Surely, that was the gentleman you mentioned when you were here before? The man who owns the car – the one you found my spectacles in?
FRAZER:	Yes, that's right. You have a very good memory, Mrs Edwards.
RUTH:	I'm afraid I've got to have! Donald never remembers a thing, if he can possibly help it. Is this Mr Denston a friend of yours?
FRAZER:	Yes. He's also a former business associate.
RUTH:	Oh, I see.
FRAZER:	Our firm came a cropper and he disappeared, owing me a great deal of money. I'm still trying to find him.
RUTH:	Well, naturally.
FRAZER:	As a matter of fact, I've taken the law into my own hands. To a certain extent, at any rate. I've just sold his car for him.
EDWARDS:	(*Chuckling*) Oh, really – good for you!
FRAZER:	I got a remarkably good price for it, too; from a man called Tupper.

There is no reaction to the name TUPPER from either of the EDWARDS.

RUTH:	Then whose car did you come down in today?

FRAZER: Oh, that's another one. I bought it this
            morning out of the proceeds. Not from Mr
            Tupper, I might add.

RUTH: Well, I do hope you manage to find your ex-
            partner, Mr Frazer. It must be infuriating
            when that sort of thing happens.

FRAZER: Oh I shall find him all right, eventually.

EDWARDS: (*Touching the print on the desk; quietly*) Oh,
            dear, if this doesn't belong to you, that
            makes it a little awkward.

FRAZER: Why?

EDWARDS: Well – I was wondering if I might borrow it
            for a little while. I'd really like time to study
            it more closely.

FRAZER: (*Laughing*) Well, I've already sold Harry's
            car, so I don't suppose lending one of his
            pictures will make much difference!

EDWARDS: That's very kind of you. I'll take good care
            of it, I assure you.

FRAZER: (*Suddenly*) But wait a minute!

*FRAZER suddenly picks up the model of the North Star from
off the desk and looks at it. EDWARDS watches him. After a
moment, FRAZER looks up and smiles.*

FRAZER: Mr Edwards, I'll strike a bargain with you.
            I'll lend you the print if you'll sell me this
            model of the North Star.

EDWARDS: (*Surprised*) Oh, well, I don't know about
            that, Mr Frazer.

FRAZER: Why? Don't you want to sell it?

EDWARDS: Oh, it isn't that, but …

FRAZER: (*Smiling*) Well, what is it?

EDWARDS: (*After a momentary hesitation*) I feel a little
            guilty about saying this after all the trouble
            you've been to on my account, but there's

an awful lot of work in these models, you know. They're rather expensive.

FRAZER: That's all right. I'll pay the market price for it.

RUTH: Oh, no, Donald, you can't accept that! After all, Mr Frazer's been very kind to us – first bringing my glasses back, and then coming all the way down here with the picture.

EDWARDS: Yes, of course, my dear, I realise that. Mr Frazer, the market price for this model would be twenty pounds. I should be more than happy to take ten for it.

FRAZER: Really? No, that's too kind. Let me pay you …

EDWARDS: No, no, I insist! Positively insist! Ten pounds, otherwise you can't have it!

FRAZER: Well, thank you very much – that's very kind of you.

RUTH picks up the model and crosses to the door.

RUTH: I'll just pop it into a box for you, Mr Frazer.

RUTH goes out. FRAZER takes out his wallet and pays EDWARDS for the model.

EDWARDS: (*Accepting the notes*) You know, I'd be delighted to let you have it for nothing, Mr Frazer, but there's so much work gone into it, one way and another – and this is almost my sole means of livelihood nowadays.

FRAZER: My dear fellow, don't be silly! I'm delighted. It's just what I need on my mantelpiece at the moment.

EDWARDS: Oh, good. (*Smiling*) Then we're both happy.

FRAZER: Yes, I had something similar on the mantelpiece a little while ago, but it disappeared.

EDWARDS: Disappeared? Do you mean it was stolen?

FRAZER: (*Looking at EDWARDS*) Well, yes – I think it was.

RUTH comes back into the room carrying a cardboard box.

RUTH: There we are! As it's not going through the post, I haven't put all the usual packing in it.

FRAZER: That's fine. (*Taking the box from RUTH*) Thank you very much.

RUTH: Now, be very careful how you carry it!

FRAZER: Don't worry, I will. (*He glances at his watch*) Well, I suppose I ought to be getting back to London. You've been very kind. I hope we shall meet again some time.

RUTH: I hope so, too, Mr Frazer. Let me get your hat and coat for you.

FRAZER and RUTH cross towards the door. EDWARDS takes a drink from his cup of tea and looks concerned. After a moment, he gets up and goes out.

CUT TO: FRAZER's Drawing Room. Night.

FRAZER has just put the box on the table and is taking off the lid. He takes the model of the North Star out of the box very carefully and examines it. After a moment he puts it on the mantelpiece and stands back, staring at it with obvious curiosity. He shakes his head, puzzled. He turns back to the empty box and picks it up. As he does so, he sees an envelope in the bottom of the box. He takes out the envelope and tears it open. Inside there is a slip of paper. He reads it. It says: Anstrov isn't dead. FRAZER stares at the note.

CUT TO: The Main Street at Henton. Day.

FRAZER's Morris Minor is parked outside The Three Bells Inn. In the distance we can see DR KILLICK strolling down the street towards the pub.

CUT TO: Inside The Three Bells. Day.

FRAZER is sitting at his old table, a drink in front of him. NORMAN GIBSON is leaning across the bar, talking to FRAZER.

NORMAN: Well, you've certainly brought better weather with you this time, Mr Frazer.

FRAZER: (*Smiling*) Yes, I must say this is the first time I've seen Henton when there wasn't a gale blowing. It looks quite different.

NORMAN: You haven't come down to meet that friend of yours again, have you? The one that didn't show up last time?

FRAZER: No – as a matter of fact I've come down to have a word with Dr Killick.

NORMAN: (*Surprised*) Dr Killick? Really?

FRAZER: Yes – I telephoned him from London. He should be here any time now.

NORMAN: Well, our Madge'll be pleased to see you, any road.

FRAZER: How is she?

NORMAN: Oh, she's fine, fine. 'Course there's not a lot to do for a young girl in this sort of town.

FRAZER: No, I suppose there isn't.

The door opens and DR KILLICK comes in.

NORMAN: Here's Dr Killick now!

KILLICK: Good evening, Mr Gibson.

NORMAN: Evening, Doctor. Here's the man you're looking for, I think.

KILLICK: Ah, yes. Mr Frazer! How are you, sir? Nice to see you again.

FRAZER and DR KILLICK shake hands.

FRAZER: Won't you sit down, Doctor?

KILLICK: Thank you.

KILLICK sits at the table facing FRAZER.

82

KILLICK:	(*Genially*) Now then – what's all this about?
FRAZER:	Will you have a drink?
KILLICK:	I won't if you don't mind. It's a little too early for me.
FRAZER:	I've got rather an odd question to ask you, Doctor. I hope you won't be offended by it.
KILLICK:	I doubt it! In twenty-five years of General Practice, I've got past being offended!
FRAZER:	Well – I hope so. (*A moment, then:*) You remember Anstrov, the Russian sailor?
KILLICK:	(*Surprised by the question*) The chap that died here? Yes, of course I remember him.
FRAZER:	Well – that's the point. That's my question, Doctor. Did he, in fact, die?
KILLICK:	I beg your pardon?
FRAZER:	I said: did he die?
KILLICK:	Yes, I heard what you said, Mr Frazer – but I'm afraid I don't understand you?
FRAZER:	I'm asking you if Anstrov was really dead?
KILLICK:	Of course he was dead!
FRAZER:	There's no doubt about it?
KILLICK:	None whatsoever!
FRAZER:	What happened to his body?

KILLICK looks at FRAZER for a moment before replying.

KILLICK:	Well, now – that <u>was</u> a little strange, if you like! It must have been after you left, I suppose. That Russian captain – what was his name again?
FRAZER:	Captain Nikiyan.
KILLICK:	That's right – Nikiyan. Well, he came back here at the head of a deputation of his men, and they insisted that Anstrov would be buried at sea.
FRAZER:	And was he?

KILLICK: Oh, yes, indeed. He was taken out in a trawler and they had a service out there.

FRAZER: Did any of the local people attend the service?

KILLICK: Oh, yes. The Vicar, Mr Deansbury, and the crew of the trawler – they were all present.

FRAZER: (*Puzzled*) I see.

KILLICK: But I don't see. I don't see the point of all this, Mr Frazer. Why are you interested in Anstrov, anyway?

FRAZER: I'm just curious.

KILLICK: Curious? Curious, about what? And isn't this a long way to come merely out of curiosity?

FRAZER: (*Shaking his head*) I was passing through Henton anyway – on my way up North.

The telephone on the bar starts to ring in the background.

KILLICK: (*Faintly annoyed*) Yes, well – I'm sorry you don't see your way to explaining your curiosity a little more fully. I can assure you I'm not in the habit of certifying a man dead when he's still alive!

NORMAN crosses to the telephone. He lifts the receiver and we hear him answering the telephone in the background.

FRAZER: I didn't mean to imply anything like that, doctor, I assure you.

NORMAN: (*In the background*) Yes, he's here. Hang on a minute, will you?

KILLICK turns expectantly, looking towards NORMAN.

NORMAN: (*Approaching from behind the bar*) It's not for you, doctor – it's for Mr Frazer. (*To FRAZER*) Telephone.

FRAZER: (*Surprised*) For me? But no one knows I'm here. Ask them who it is, will you?

FRAZER gets up from his bench and moves towards the bar.
NORMAN returns and picks up the receiver.

NORMAN: (*Into the phone*) Who's that speaking,
            please?

FRAZER has reached the bar and is looking at NORMAN.

NORMAN: (*Turning: to FRAZER*) It's a Mr Denston. A
            Mr Harry Denston.

End of Episode Three

Episode Four

OPEN TO: The Saloon Bar of the Three Bells pub. Day.
DR KILLICK is sitting at a table. FRASER is standing.
NORMAN is behind the bar holding the phone.
NORMAN: It's Mr Denston. Mr Harry Denston.
FRAZER takes the receiver.
FRAZER: (*On the phone*) Hello? Tim Frazer speaking
             …
HARRY's VOICE: Tim … this is Harry …
FRAZER: Harry, I've been looking all over the place
             for you! Where are you?
HARRY: Tim, listen …
FRAZER: Where the hell are you? Why didn't you
             turn up here last week?
HARRY: Look, Tim, there's no point in losing your
             temper. I couldn't help it last week. I
             couldn't get down to Henton. Now please
             listen to me.
FRAZER: Go on. I'm listening.
HARRY: You've got to stop chasing around after me!
             You've got to forget I exist! Do you
             understand?
FRAZER: What do you mean – forget you exist? You
             owe me money, Harry – a great deal of
             money!
HARRY: (*Hesitantly*) Is it the money that's worrying
             you?
FRAZER: Of course it's the money that's worrying
             me! I need every penny I can lay my hands
             on! Look, I've got to see you, Harry! We've
             got things to talk about! It's important!
HARRY: (*After a pause*) All right. I'll see you …
FRAZER: When?
HARRY: Next Sunday morning …
FRAZER: Where?

HARRY:	At your flat. I'll be there about nine-thirty.
FRAZER:	Can I depend on this?
HARRY:	Yes but listen! If you tell anyone about this – if you breathe a word about it – I shan't turn up. Do you understand?
FRAZER:	(*Irritated*) Yes, I understand.
HARRY:	I'm serious …
FRAZER:	I'm hoping we're both serious, Harry. Nine-thirty Sunday morning – and be there this time!

FRAZER replaces the receiver and stands for a moment deep in thought. KILLICK and NORMAN are watching him.

FRAZER:	I'm sorry about that interruption, doctor. It was an old friend of mine.
KILLICK:	I must apologise if I seemed irritable just now.
FRAZER:	(*Sitting at the table*) There's no need for an apology, your comments were more than justified. I shouldn't have asked such a ridiculous question.
KILLICK:	While you were on the telephone, I was thinking about what you said …
FRAZER:	About the possibility of Anstrov not being dead?
KILLICK:	Yes. (*With a little laugh*) It's an extraordinary suggestion! Quite extraordinary! Whatever put such an idea into your head?
FRAZER:	(*Evasively; wishing to change the subject*) Oh, it was just a thought, doctor. It occurred to me one day when I was thinking about Henton and the storm, and what happened down here.

KILLICK:	Yes, but someone must have said something to you about Anstrov, or you must have read something about him. I mean, you don't ask a doctor a question like that without a definite reason.
FRAZER:	(*With a little laugh*) No, I suppose not. (*Nodding*) I have a reason.
KILLICK:	Well, it must be a very good one.
FRAZER:	Yes, I think perhaps it is.

A pause.

KILLICK:	But you're not going to tell me what it is?
FRAZER:	I can't. (*Smiling*) Not for the moment, at any rate.
KILLICK:	Well – you've made me very curious. Very curious, to say the least. (*He rises*) How long are you planning to stay with us this time?
FRAZER:	I'm going up to Carlisle tomorrow to see some friends.
KILLICK:	Then back to London?
FRAZER:	Yes.
KILLICK:	I'm treating myself to a trip to London in a few days' time.
FRAZER:	Oh really – well here's my address. I'd be delighted if you'd drop in and see me.
KILLICK:	I may take you up on that. But I expect I shall be pretty busy. So many people to see – you know what London is.
FRAZER:	Yes, I do indeed. Well, I think I'd better go upstairs and unpack. Thank you for sparing the time to see me. Goodbye, doctor.

FRAZER goes up the staircase. KILLICK crosses to the bar.

KILLICK:	Give me a packet of cigarettes, Norman – the usual. (*NORMAN gives him a packet*) Thank you. (*He pays for them*) Mr Frazer sounded excited I thought – on the telephone.
NORMAN:	Yes – and do you know why?
KILLICK:	No?
NORMAN:	That was the chap he was supposed to meet here last week. Harry Denston. According to our Madge, he owes Mr Frazer thousands.
KILLICK:	Oh! Oh, well that probably accounts for it. I get excited myself when anyone owes me a fiver. Goodbye.
NORMAN:	Goodbye, doctor.

KILLICK crosses, picks up his bag from the table and goes out.

CUT TO: The Drawing Room of FRAZER's Flat. Sunday: a bright sunny morning.

MRS GLOVER, the daily woman, is tidying the room. After a moment FRAZER comes out of the bedroom. He is wearing a dressing gown.

MRS GLOVER:	I'm just about finished now, sir.
FRAZER:	(*Faintly irritated*) Good. There was really no need to come in this morning, Mrs Glover.
MRS GLOVER:	If I don't come in of a Sunday, it only means extra work of a Monday, sir.
FRAZER:	Yes, well – you'd better finish off now. I'm expecting someone.
MRS GLOVER:	I'll just have a dust round the bedroom before I go.
FRAZER:	No – leave that. It can wait till tomorrow.

The doorbell rings.

MRS GLOVER: That'll be your friend now, sir.

FRAZER: Yes, let him in as you go out, would you, Mrs Glover?

MRS GLOVER: Rightio, sir, and I'll see you tomorrow.

MRS GLOVER picks up her hat and coat from a chair and goes out. FRAZER stands waiting impatiently. MRS GLOVER returns with HELEN. FRAZER changes his expression as he sees HELEN.

MRS GLOVER: It's Miss Baker, sir.

HELEN comes into the room. MRS GLOVER goes, closing the door behind her.

HELEN: Hello, Tim.

FRAZER: Helen! I didn't expect you this morning!

HELEN: No – I know you didn't.

FRAZER: (*Glancing at his watch; worried*) Look, I don't want to seem inhospitable, but I'm expecting someone this morning, and it's just about …

HELEN: (*Quietly*) It's all right, Tim, I know all about it. (*She takes off her fur stole and moves towards TIM*) You're expecting Harry.

FRAZER: (*Surprised; quietly*) How did you know?

HELEN: I've seen him. I saw him on Friday night. He told me to tell you that he won't be coming this morning.

FRAZER: (*Angrily*) Why? Why isn't he coming?

HELEN: I don't know. He just told me to deliver the message to you.

FRAZER: (*Taking hold of HELEN's arm*) Where is he, Helen? Where's he staying?

HELEN: I don't know. I just can't make it out, Tim. He telephoned me on Friday and

93

	asked me to meet him at a café near Broxbourne. I drove down there after the show.
FRAZER:	What sort of café?
HELEN:	Oh, it was a dreadful place. A pull in for lorry drivers. I think it was called Ma's Place.
FRAZER:	But why on earth meet you at a dump like that?
HELEN:	I don't know. It wasn't my idea, I can assure you. I tried to persuade him to come to the flat, but he wouldn't.
FRAZER:	Go on, Helen. What happened?
HELEN:	He said he'd spoken to you and that you were very annoyed about the money he owed you.
FRAZER:	I pretended to be a great deal more annoyed than I am, because I wanted to see him.
HELEN:	Yes, I realised that. Anyway, he said he wasn't going to see you and he told me to pay you back. He gave me the money. (*She opens her bag and takes out a cheque*)
FRAZER:	He gave you the money!
HELEN:	Yes – five thousand pounds.
FRAZER:	But where would Harry get five thousand pounds from?
HELEN:	I don't know. (*Tensely; faintly on edge*) All I can tell you, darling, is that he gave me the money.

FRAZER takes the cheque from HELEN and looks at it.

FRAZER:	(*Quietly; looking up at HELEN*) But this is your cheque.

94

HELEN: Yes, I know.

FRAZER: This looks to me like the old trick, Helen. Trying to repay Harry's debts with your own money.

HELEN: No, it isn't, Tim, I swear it isn't! He paid me the money in five pound notes – obviously I didn't want to carry that much money about with me, so I put it in the bank.

FRAZER: You know, I find this very hard to believe, Helen.

HELEN: Darling, I can only tell you the truth!

FRAZER: (*Looking at the cheque again*) How on earth would Harry raise five thousand pounds?

HELEN: Perhaps he borrowed it from somebody; I don't know! That was always a favourite game of Harry's – borrowing from Peter to pay Paul.

FRAZER: (*Angrily*) Why doesn't he want to see me?

HELEN is about to reply, then hesitates.

FRAZER: Come on, Helen, why won't he see me?

HELEN: He's just started a new business with someone, and he doesn't want them to know about the past – about your partnership breaking up and the firm going bust.

FRAZER: Well, that's the most unlikely story I've heard yet – even from Harry! The whole world knew about our firm going into liquidation! We had a very good notice in the Financial Times! Remember!

HELEN: Yes, well maybe he feels that you'd talk about it – or interfere, or something.

FRAZER: Is that likely? In spite of everything Harry
              and I have always been very good friends.
              You know that, Helen.

HELEN: Yes, I know that, Tim – but what can I do
              about it? I told him what you said the other
              day, that it was desperately important that
              you see him. He just wouldn't listen.

The doorbell rings.

FRAZER: (*With a little nod*) I see.

*FRAZER puts the cheque down on the table and moves
towards the hall.*

FRAZER: Excuse me, Helen.

*FRAZER goes out into the hall leaving the drawing room
door open.*

CUT TO: The Hall of FRAZER's Flat. Day.

*FRAZER opens the front door. There is a collection of
Sunday newspapers on the mat. He picks up the papers and
is closing the door when his eye catches a reflection in the
hall mirror. He stands looking at the mirror. In the mirror
we can see HELEN in the drawing room. She is standing in
front of the mantelpiece, a tiny Minox camera in her hand,
taking a photograph of the model of the North Star. She
quickly replaces the camera in her handbag and moves
away from the mantelpiece. FRAZER closes the front door
and returns to the drawing room.*

CUT TO: The Drawing Room of FRAZER's Flat. Day.

*FRAZER returns and puts the newspapers down on the
table.*

FRAZER: I never asked you to have a drink.

HELEN: It's too early, darling. (*She picks up her
              stole*) I'm afraid I must be going, I've got
              some people coming to lunch.

FRAZER picks up the cheque and looks at it again.

FRAZER: Helen, before I accept this, you swear that Harry really did give you the money?

HELEN: Yes, of course! Do you think I've got five thousand pounds to give away?

FRAZER: (*Folding the cheque*) Well, if Harry wants it this way – that's the end of a beautiful friendship. He's entitled to ruin his own life, I suppose. How about you, Helen? Are you seeing him again?

HELEN: I don't know.

FRAZER: You're still engaged, I take it?

HELEN: I don't know about that, either. We weren't particularly friendly when we met on Friday. (*She moves towards the door*) Tim, I must fly! Let's have lunch together one day soon – this week, if possible.

FRAZER: Yes, all right. I'll give you a ring.

They both cross into the hall.

CUT TO: The Hall of FRAZER's Flat. Day.

FRAZER: How's the show going?

HELEN: We're coming off next week. Didn't you know?

FRAZER: Oh, I'm sorry.

HELEN: I'm not, darling. I shall be glad of the rest.

HELEN goes out of the front door. FRAZER returns to the drawing room.

CUT TO: The Drawing room of FRAZER's Flat. Day.

FRAZER enters and walks to the sofa and stands staring at the model of the North Star.

CUT TO: Ma's Place on the Waltham Crossroads. Day.

This is a transport café of the worst type. There is a large drive in and a small wooden shack covered with tin advertisements.

FRAZER's car pulls up in front of the shack and he gets out. He crosses towards the door of the café.

CUT TO: Inside MA's Place. Day

A small hut, squalid establishment with dull tables and a counter at the back on which stands a tea urn and a display of turned up sandwiches under a glass case.

MA DODSWORTH herself is sitting behind the counter reading a Sunday newspaper. FRAZER comes in the door and crosses to the counter.

MA: Yes, love?

FRAZER: A cup of tea, please.

MA: Sugar?

FRAZER: Thank you.

MA: (*Efficiently; at the urn*) One tea with. (*She turns to pour the tea*)

FRAZER: You're very quiet today.

MA: We liven up later, love. Be busy tonight. One tea with – fourpence.

FRAZER: I wonder if you would help me?

MA puts the cup down in front of FRAZER.

MA: Anything I can do. Always happy to oblige a gentleman.

FRAZER: Well, I wondered if you'd remember a lady coming in here, the night before last?

MA: A lady? We don't get many of them, love. Night before last? Let me see now – that'd be Friday, of course. Oh, yes! I remember. There was a lady come in here on Friday night – had a coffee. Very high class altogether, she was. Nice with it, mind – but very high class.

FRAZER: Did she meet anyone?

MA: Yes, now you come to mention it, she did. A gentleman. One of my regulars.

FRAZER: (*Surprised*) One of your regulars?

MA: That's right, love. Often pops in for a cup of tea and a sandwich. Surprised he hasn't been in this afternoon as a matter of fact.

FRAZER: Does he live round here?

MA: I can't say, dearie. Never ask questions about your clientele – that's my motto.

FRAZER: Yes, of course. (*Drinks his tea*) You say he often drops in?

MA: (*Busy at the urn*) Yes, he was in almost every day this last week. (*Turning*) If you was to sit down and enjoy your cup of tea in peace, you'll probably see him. This is just about his time.

FRAZER looks at MA for a moment, then picks up his cup.

FRAZER: Thanks – I'll do that.

FRAZER crosses and sits at one of the tables. After a moment MA wanders into a small recess at the back of the counter. She is out of sight of FRAZER. There is a telephone there. MA goes to it and dials a number. She sits for a few moments as it rings out. The receiver is lifted at the other end. We hear – but do not see – TUPPER.

TUPPER: (*On the other end of the line*) Broxbourne 5101.

MA: (*Softly*) This is Ma. He's here, and I've done what you said.

TUPPER: Good. All right, Ma.

There is a click as the receiver is replaced at the other end. MA casually strolls back to the counter. FRAZER is still sitting at the table, sipping his tea. MA takes up the newspaper again and pretends to read.

CUT TO: Outside MA's Place Café. Day.

FRAZER's Morris is still parked outside.

CUT TO: Inside MA's Place. Day.

FRAZER is sitting at the table with his teacup empty in front of him. He stubs out a cigarette end, looks at his watch, then he looks towards the counter. There is no sign of MA. At that moment the door opens and a YOUNG MAN enters. In his way he is dressed smartly with a short white raincoat, narrow trousers, pointed Italian shoes, and a soft hat. He has fair hair and a faintly effeminate manner. He walks over to FRAZER's table and sits down opposite him. For a moment he says nothing, but stares at FRAZER, smiling slightly. FRAZER ignores LESTER but is aware of his presence at the table.

LESTER: You're Frazer, aren't you?

FRAZER: That's right. I'm Frazer. Who are you?

LESTER: You can call me Lester.

FRAZER: Thank you very much – Lester.

LESTER: In case you're interested – I'm a friend of a friend of yours.

FRAZER: Who is this friend?

LESTER: Harry Denston.

FRAZER: (*After a moment*) I'm interested.

LESTER: (*With a smile*) Yes, I thought you would be.

FRAZER: What is it you want?

LESTER: Well, I don't know that I want anything in particular. I'd just like to give you a piece of advice, that's all.

FRAZER: Go ahead. But perhaps I'd better warn you, I'm not very good at taking advice – particularly from strangers.

LESTER: That's all right, Mr Frazer. (*Still smiling*) That's all right. You don't have to take it.

A slight pause. LESTER continues to smile.

FRAZER: (*Faintly irritated*) Well, Lester, what is this advice of yours?

LESTER: We want you to stop looking for Harry Denston.

FRAZER: Why?

LESTER: Because you're making him nervous – very nervous. We don't like it.

FRAZER: Who's we?

LESTER: Harry and me.

FRAZER: Let's get this straight. Who is it I'm making nervous, Harry or you?

LESTER: It's Harry. You don't worry me. It takes a lot to make me nervous.

FRAZER: (*Quietly*) Yes, I can imagine that.

LESTER: (*Rising*) Well, that's the advice. I hope you'll take it. I know I would, if I was in your shoes.

FRAZER: (*Looking up at LESTER*) Would you?

LESTER: I certainly would. After all, why be a sucker? Harry's paid you the money he owed you. (*A shrug*) You're in clover, why should you worry?

FRAZER: I'm not worried; I'm just curious, that's all.

LESTER: Yes, well stop being curious, chum. It'll pay you in the end. (*Smiling; A sudden thought*) D'you know what I'd do, if I was you?

FRAZER: No, tell me, Lester.

LESTER: I'd take a nice little trip to the South of France – Monte Carlo, Nice, Cannes, Juan-les-Pins – the lot!

FRAZER: Surely, it's the wrong time of the year for the South of France?

LESTER: (*Smiling*) Not for you, it isn't.

There is a pause. FRAZER continues to look at LESTER.

FRAZER: (*Non-committally*) I'll think about it.

LESTER: Yes, well don't think about it too long, chum. (*He turns and crosses towards the door*) Cheerio!

FRAZER: (*As LESTER reaches the door*) Lester …

LESTER: (*Stopping; turning*) Yes?

FRAZER: You forgot to tell me something.

LESTER: What?

FRAZER: What happens if I don't go to the South of France?

LESTER: (*Unsmiling: after a tiny pause*) What happened to Crombie?

LESTER turns and goes out, closing the door behind him.

CUT TO: FRAZER's Drawing Room. Day.

The telephone is ringing. It goes on ringing for a good time. FRAZER enters. He goes to the phone and answers it.

FRAZER: Sloane 0181 …

We hear CHARLES ROSS on the other end of the line.

ROSS: Frazer?

FRAZER: Yes …

CUT TO: ROSS's Office. Day.

ROSS: This is Ross. I want to ask you something.

FRAZER: Go ahead.

ROSS: Can you remember the suit Crombie was wearing – the last time you saw him.

CUT TO: FRAZER's Drawing Room. Day.

FRAZER: Yes. It was a grey lounge suit.

ROSS: Single breasted?

FRAZER: Yes – single breasted …

ROSS: Thank you.

FRAZER: Why do you want to know about the suit?

CUT TO: ROSS's Office. Day.

ROSS: The police have found a body in Epping Forest; it's unrecognisable – but we think it might be Crombie.

CUT TO: FRAZER's Drawing Room. Day.

FRAZER: I see.

ROSS: Thank you, Frazer.

FRAZER replaces the receiver. He removes his coat slowly, thinking of CROMBIE. The doorbell rings. FRAZER goes out to the hall.

CUT TO: The Hall of FRAZER's Flat. Day.

FRAZER opens the front door. We see DR KILLICK.

KILLICK: Good evening, Mr Frazer!

FRAZER: Good evening, doctor. How nice to see you.

KILLICK: I took you at your word, you see.

FRAZER: I'm glad you did – through here.

They pass to the drawing room.

CUT TO: The Drawing Room of FRAZER's Flat. Day.

FRAZER: Let me take your coat, doctor.

KILLICK: No, no, I'm not staying, I haven't really got much time, Mr Frazer. But I didn't want to go back to Henton without seeing you.

FRAZER: What time is your train?

KILLICK: I think it's a quarter to seven, but I'm not sure. I'm always frightfully hazy about trains, I'm afraid.

FRAZER: Well – you've got time for a drink anyway. (*Crosses to the drinks table*) What would you like? Sherry? Whisky and soda?

KILLICK: Do you happen to have a brandy and soda, by any chance?

103

FRAZER: Yes, of course.

KILLICK: Well – er – just a spot of soda, Mr Frazer.

FRAZER mixes the drinks. As KILLICK sits he looks round the room, amongst other things the model ship on the mantelpiece. FRAZER brings the doctor his drink.

FRAZER: There you are, doctor. When did you arrive?

KILLICK: Yesterday morning – and I seem to have been on the go the whole time. The extraordinary thing is I haven't done half what I intended to do.

FRAZER: (*Laughing*) That's always the case. Cheers!

The DOCTOR raises his glass. FRAZER smiles at him.

FRAZER: It's nice to see you again, doctor. How are things in Henton?

KILLICK: Oh, pretty much the same. Nothing very exciting ever happens at Henton, you know.

FRAZER: (*Amused*) Now you can't tell me that!

KILLICK: (*Laughing*) Oh, that Russian affair was an exception – you can't go by that!

FRAZER: No, I suppose not. Still, I'll bet the local people won't forget it in a hurry.

KILLICK: Forget it? My dear fellow, they'll never stop talking about it – not in a hundred years! But still, who am I to criticise? I've been dining out on it ever since. (*He laughs and drinks his Brandy; looks at FRAZER*) You know, I've often thought of our last little chat together, Mr Frazer.

FRAZER: Have you, Doctor?

KILLICK: Yes – you asked me about Anstrov; whether he was dead or not.

FRAZER: (*Pleasantly*) Yes, I remember. (*Trying to change the subject*) Let me get you another brandy, doctor.

104

KILLICK: No. No, thank you. (*Smiling*) Mr Frazer, I know, for some reason or other, you don't want to tell me why you asked that question, but – (*With a little laugh*) do you think you could satisfy just part of my curiosity? Whoever put such an idea into your head in the first place?

FRAZER: No one put it into my head. I just thought of it. It was quite an original thought, doctor. (*Smiling*) If a little crazy.

KILLICK: Yes, well – (*He rises; looks at FRAZER for a moment*) I know this will surprise you, but – I'm not so sure now whether it was crazy or not.

FRAZER: What do you mean?

KILLICK: Well – (*He hesitates*) You asked me if Anstrov was dead.

FRAZER: Yes.

KILLICK: (*Looking at the glass in his hand*) The answer to your question could be – no, Mr Frazer. (*Looking up*) Let me explain. I certified that a man named Anstrov died at Henton.

FRAZER: Yes …

KILLICK: Well – what proof have we that the dead man was Anstrov?

FRAZER: There was his belongings, and Captain Nikiyan identified the body.

KILLICK: Yes, and that's all. But I'll tell you something; something rather interesting. The rest of the crew didn't know Anstrov very well.

FRAZER: How do you know?

KILLICK: They all signed on at Archangel. But Anstrov didn't join the ship until they reached Gdynia in Poland.

FRAZER: Who told you this?

105

KILLICK: One of the nurses at the hospital, she'd been talking to the First Mate. (*With a smile*) You see, you made me rather curious, Mr Frazer – so I made one or two enquiries of my own.

FRAZER: (*Thoughtfully*) Yes, so I see. Still, it's only a theory, isn't it, doctor?

KILLICK: Yes, indeed, it's only a theory. But it's one answer to your question. Now I really must be making a move.

As KILLICK turns he looks at the model of the North Star.

KILLICK: That's a very attractive little model you've got there.

FRAZER: Yes, I'm rather fond of it myself.

KILLICK: I've always been fascinated by those things. I remember when I was a student there was a little shop in the same street as my digs that used to specialise in models. Ships, aircraft, all sorts of things.

FRAZER: Was that in London?

KILLICK: Oh, yes, in Church Street. What was the name of the shop now? Bonnington's. That was it – Bonnington's. I always used to covet the models they had in the window. (*He sighs*) It's all a very long time ago. (*He turns towards the hall*) Well, thank you again for the drink, Mr Frazer. I certainly needed it!

FRAZER: I'll see you out.

They both cross towards the hall.

CUT TO: The High Street of Cobham.

A car draws to a standstill outside a grocer's shop and RUTH EDWARDS gets out of it and goes into the shop. We see that FRAZER's car is parked on a corner on the other side of the road. FRAZER gets out and crosses to RUTH's car. He bends and looks through the window, then he quickly opens the door, and gets into the front passenger seat.

FRAZER looks round inside the car. He notices a long stuffed ornamental tiger on the shelf behind the back seat and smiles to himself. On the back seat he sees a square brown paper parcel – similar to the one in which he was given the model. He picks it up and looks at the name and address on it – it is stamped and ready for posting. We get a close up of the label on the parcel. It reads: Bonnington, Esq., 48 Clayton Road, Camden Town, London NW1.

FRAZER puts the parcel back on the seat. As he does so the door is opened by RUTH EDWARDS. She stops on seeing FRAZER.

FRAZER: (*Quietly*) Do get in, Mrs Edwards. I'd like to talk to you.

RUTH hesitates for a moment and then gets into the driving seat. She is obviously nervous.

RUTH: Mr Frazer – what are you doing in my car?

FRAZER: I want to have a talk with you.

RUTH: Well why on earth didn't you come to the cottage, Mr Frazer?

FRAZER: I didn't think you'd like that somehow. I had my reasons.

RUTH: (*Apparently puzzled*) What is it you want?

FRAZER: (*Pleasantly*) Well, first of all – thank you for the note.

RUTH: Note? I'm afraid I don't understand you?

FRAZER: I'm referring to the note that was with the model I bought from your husband.

RUTH: I'm sorry; I really don't know what you're talking about! Now, if you'll excuse me …

107

FRAZER: Wait a moment! I apologise. I've obviously made a mistake. It must have been your husband who put the note in the box. I'll have a word with him about it.

FRAZER turns, as if to leave the car.

RUTH: No, wait! (*A pause; quietly*) There's no need to tell Donald about this. What is it you want to know?

FRAZER: Was it you that sent the note?

RUTH: (*After a moment of hesitation*) Yes.

FRAZER: Why?

RUTH: I thought it might help you, that's all.

FRAZER: Help me? In what way?

RUTH: (*Glancing out of the window*) Look, we can't talk here! It's quite impossible!

FRAZER: (*Determined to talk; with obvious authority*) Help me – in what way? To find Harry Denston?

RUTH: Yes.

FRAZER: The note said "Anstrov isn't dead". What did you mean by that? That the dead man wasn't Anstrov?

RUTH: Yes. (*A note of desperation in her voice; looking out of the window again*) Mr Frazer, I'm sorry, but I just can't talk to you now! I'm expecting my husband at any moment, and if he sees us together, he'll …

FRAZER: All right, if I go now, will you meet me tomorrow some time?

RUTH: (*Hesitating*) Well, I don't know but … (*Suddenly; making a decision*) Yes, I'll see you at the cottage about eleven o'clock …

FRAZER: Good. I'll be there.

RUTH: No, wait a minute! Donald's going up to Town
            for the day, I think he's catching the eleven
            o'clock train – so you'd better make it half
            past, just to be on the safe side.
FRAZER: All right. (*He turns to get out of the car then
            hesitates*) Oh – before I go, there's something I
            want to ask you. Do you know a Dr Killick, by
            any chance?
RUTH: Dr Killick? No. Why do you ask?
FRAZER: It was Dr Killick who first made me realise
            what your note meant. I wondered if he was a
            friend of yours.
RUTH: (*Looking out of the window*) No, I'm sorry, I've
            never heard of him.
FRAZER: (*Quietly opening the car door*) I'll see you
            tomorrow then.

*FRAZER goes out of shot. RUTH looks after him, then starts
the engine.*

CUT TO: A Shop Window in Camden Town. Day.
The window, although fairly tidy, contains an odd
assortment of articles – stamp albums, fishing rods, roller
skates, playing cards, guitars, and one or two models of
ships similar to those made by DONALD EDWARDS.
*FRAZER is standing and looking in the window. He surveys
the contents for a moment, then goes towards the shop door.*
CUT TO: Inside the Shop. Day.
*FRAZER comes in the front door. He goes to the counter. At
the other end of the counter a middle-aged man is serving a
woman who is choosing a photograph album.*
CUSTOMER: It looks awfully nice, I must say, but will
            these things hold the snaps in properly?
MAN: Oh, yes, we've sold a lot of this type just
            recently.

CUSTOMER: Well – I don't know. The last one I had was an awful nuisance – they all kept falling out.

MAN: Well, perhaps you'd like to think about it for a bit, while I just attend to this gentleman.

HE smiles and moves across to where FRAZER is standing.

MAN: Yes, sir? What can I do for you?

FRAZER: I'm rather interested in the models you have in the window.

MAN: Oh, yes, sir? Any particular one that's caught your fancy?

FRAZER: Well, actually, I'm looking for a model of a particular ship, a frigate called the North Star.

The MAN smiles and nods. He opens a drawer under the counter and takes out a small envelope which he gives to FRAZER.

MAN: You're on time, anyway. It only arrived this morning.

He nods to FRAZER and turns back to his lady CUSTOMER.

MAN: Well, what do you think, madam?

CUSTOMER: Well – I don't know, I'm sure. Have you got any others I can look at?

FRAZER stands for a moment, looks at the MAN, then he turns on his heels and goes out of the shop.

CUT TO: Outside the Shop. Day.

FRAZER walks towards his car, the envelope in his hand. When he gets to the car he stops and looks at the envelope. He hesitates and glances up and down the street to see if anyone is watching him, then he rips open the envelope and takes out a small envelope.

CUT TO: The Hall of FRAZER's Flat. Night.

The front doorbell is ringing. FRAZER crosses to the front
door. HELEN is standing there.

HELEN: Hello, Tim!

FRAZER: Come in, Helen.

HELEN: You sounded very serious on the phone.
           What's all this about a surprise? I hope it's a
           nice one.

FRAZER: That's for you to decide.

They cross to the drawing room.

CUT TO: FRAZER's Drawing Room. Night.

HELEN and FRAZER enter.

FRAZER: Sit down, Helen.

FRAZER takes out his wallet and extracts a photograph.

FRAZER: There you are. It's come out rather well, hasn't
           it? I congratulate you on your photography.

HELEN: Oh, Tim!

FRAZER: I think I deserve an explanation, Helen. And
           don't try and tell me you didn't take the
           photograph, because I saw you.

HELEN: (*Rising*) I don't know what to say.

FRAZER: Why did you take that photograph? I want to
           know!

HELEN: Harry asked me to do it. He gave me the
           camera –

FRAZER: Helen, I want the truth!

HELEN: I'm telling you the truth! I just didn't think.
           Harry gave me the camera and asked me to take
           a photograph of the model on your
           mantelpiece. There just didn't seem to be any
           reason why I shouldn't take it, so – Tim, I'm
           sorry I should have told you about it. I realise
           that now.

111

FRAZER: Did he tell you why he wanted the photograph?
HELEN: No.
FRAZER: Have you any idea why he wanted it?
HELEN: No, of course I haven't!
FRAZER: I don't believe you. These people – the people
            that Harry's mixed up with – are not playing a
            game, Helen. If you know anything about them,
            anything at all – you'd better tell me. And
            you'd better tell me now, before it's too late.
HELEN: What do you mean – before it's too late?
FRAZER: I told you what happened to that friend of mine.
            I found him out there, in the hall, with a knife
            in his back. Now what happened when you saw
            Harry?
HELEN: I've told you.
FRAZER: Tell me again!
HELEN: (*Not looking at FRAZER*) He said he wanted
            you to leave him alone. He gave me the money
            – the five thousand pounds – and then he asked
            me to take the photograph. He told me to post
            the camera to a shop in Church Street.
FRAZER: Bonnington's?
HELEN: (*Turns*) Yes, that's right – but how did you
            know about Bonnington's?
FRAZER: Helen, what did Harry look like?
HELEN: He looked ill, and frightened. He wouldn't talk
            about anything, except that – He just wants you
            to leave him alone, Tim.
FRAZER: Then why did he write and ask me to meet him
            at Henton?
HELEN: I don't know.
FRAZER: Did he mention Henton, or the letter?
HELEN: No.

FRAZER: Did he tell you where he got the five thousand pounds from?

HELEN: No. I've told you – he told me nothing!

The telephone rings. FRAZER picks up the receiver. The voice on the other end of the line is RUTH EDWARDS.

FRAZER: Sloane 0181 …

RUTH: Mr Frazer?

FRAZER: Yes. Who is that please?

RUTH: This is Ruth Edwards …

FRAZER: Oh, hello …

RUTH: My husband's catching a later train tomorrow morning, Mr Frazer – so please don't get here until after one o'clock.

FRAZER: Yes, all right.

RUTH: You understand?

FRAZER: Yes, I understand. Thank you for ringing.

CUT TO: A Country Road. Day.

FRAZER's car is driving along the road.

CUT TO: A Road near Cobham, Surrey. Day.

There has been an accident and a badly smashed car is upside down in a ditch by the road. There are two police cars and an ambulance pulled up nearby and a couple of passing motorists have stopped. There are about a half a dozen passers-by looking on.

FRAZER's car pulls up at the blockage of traffic, and he puts his head out of the window to see what the hold-up is. As he does so a POLICEMAN walks past him going towards the police car.

FRAZER: What's the matter, officer?

P.C.: I'm afraid there's been an accident, sir.

FRAZER: Anyone badly hurt?

P.C.:   Only one, sir. They're just getting her out now.
           I think she's had it, though.

The POLICEMAN moves on. FRAZER watches as a stretcher is taken over to the wrecked car. Suddenly he notices a boy of about thirteen standing near the car. He is holding a stuffed toy tiger and is showing it to his friend, a slightly younger boy. FRAZER gets out of his car and joins them.

FRAZER: Where did you get that from, sonny?

BOY: It came out of the car. (*He points towards the wreck*) The one what was smashed up …

FRAZER nods to the boy, and crosses to the small group around the wrecked car. He speaks to the POLICEMAN.

FRAZER: Excuse me, but have you identified the lady yet?

P.C.:   No, we haven't had a chance yet, sir.

FRAZER: I wonder if I could see her for a moment? I think she's a friend of mine.

P.C.:   Oh – this way, sir.

The POLICEMAN pushes his way through the crowd and FRAZER follows. On the ground, by the wrecked car, a woman is lying on the stretcher, swathed in blankets. The ambulance men take up the stretcher and start to carry it towards the ambulance. The camera tracks in on the woman. It is RUTH EDWARDS.

End of Episode Four

Episode Five

OPEN TO: A country road outside of Cobham, Surrey. A crowd is gathered near RUTH EDWARDS' car which is overturned in the ditch.

At the centre of the crowd, RUTH EDWARDS is lying on a stretcher. FRAZER is kneeling beside her. The AMBULANCE MEN finish their preparations, lift the stretcher, and force their way through the crowd with it. FRAZER follows.

When the men reach the ambulance they open the doors and put the stretcher inside.

A doctor (DR HARRIS) and a POLICEMAN are talking beside the ambulance. FRAZER approaches them. He speaks to the POLICEMAN.

FRAZER: Excuse me …

POLICEMAN: Yes, sir?

FRAZER: This lady's a friend of mine. Her name's Ruth Edwards. I wonder if I could go with her to the hospital?

POLICEMAN: (*Puzzled*) You weren't involved in the accident, were you, sir?

FRAZER: No – I just happened to be passing.

POLICEMAN: Oh, I see. Well, you'd better ask the doctor here.

The POLICEMAN indicates the DOCTOR with a nod of his head.

FRAZER: (*To the DOCTOR*) Will that be all right, doctor?

HARRIS: Yes – I should think so; as long as you don't get in the way. I can't tell until I examine her at the hospital, but she seems to be pretty badly hurt.

FRAZER: Will she – live?

HARRIS: I don't know, sir. I can't say yet. Well – let's go, shall we?

117

FRAZER and the DOCTOR get into the ambulance and the DRIVER closes the doors.

CUT TO: Inside the Ambulance. Day.
RUTH EDWARDS is on the stretcher, semi-conscious. FRAZER is sitting on the pull-out at the front of the ambulance. He is looking intently at RUTH. DR HARRIS has his back to FRAZER and is taking instruments out of his bag which is on the other stretcher.
RUTH EDWARDS opens her eyes and looks at FRAZER. Her mouth forms words but no sound comes forth. FRAZER leans closer to her.

FRAZER: (*Quietly*) What is it, Mrs Edwards?
RUTH: Helen Baker …
FRAZER: Yes, what about Helen?
RUTH: … She didn't see Denston …
FRAZER: (*Puzzled*) She didn't see him?
RUTH: (*Trying to shake her head*) No. She was … lying … She didn't … see … Denston.
FRAZER: (*Intently*) Where is Harry Denston?
RUTH tries to speak again, but for the moment words fail her.
FRAZER: Try to tell me. This is very important, Mrs Edwards. Where is Harry Denston?
The DOCTOR turns and looks at FRAZER, curious. FRAZER leans very close to RUTH, waiting for her to speak.
RUTH: (*After a moment*) I … Helen knows …
RUTH closes her eyes. FRAZER looks at the DOCTOR who shakes his head.
FRAZER stands up and DR HARRIS turns towards RUTH with a hypodermic in his hand.

CUT TO: The Road. Day.

The ambulance is racing along the road.

CUT TO: FRAZER's Drawing Room. Day.

FRAZER is sitting at his desk. The doorbell rings. He gets up and goes through into the hall.

CUT TO: The Hall of FRAZER's Flat. Day.

FRAZER opens the front door. DR KILLICK is standing there.

FRAZER: Well, do come in!

KILLICK: Thank you.

FRAZER: Dr Killick! Good gracious! I thought you were back in the wilds of Yorkshire by now!

KILLICK: As a matter of fact I've been there and back since I saw you last, Mr Frazer.

DR KILLICK enters and FRAZER closes the door behind him.

KILLICK: I hope you don't mind my calling unexpectedly like this?

FRAZER: Not at all! Delighted to see you, doctor.

FRAZER and the DOCTOR go through to the drawing room.

CUT TO: FRAZER's Drawing Room. Day.

KILLICK: I've just got in from Henton and was on my way to the Royal Hospital. I thought I'd kill two birds with one stone.

FRAZER: Oh, yes?

KILLICK: I was in The Three Bells at Henton last night, and Norman Gibson, the landlord, happened to mention that a letter had arrived for you from London. He was going to send it on, but since I

119

was coming down here, I offered to deliver it for him.

FRAZER: That was very kind of you, doctor. Will you excuse me one moment? Please sit down.

KILLICK: Yes, of course.

FRAZER looks at the envelope then rips it open. He reads the letter then replaces it inside the envelope.

FRAZER: It's from that friend of mine, Harry Denston.

KILLICK: The man you were supposed to meet at Henton?

FRAZER: Yes. I can't imagine why he wrote to The Three Bells. He's got my address. (*He puts the letter in his pocket*) Enough of that. What about some coffee – I've got a percolator on out there at the moment.

KILLICK: No, I don't think I will, if you don't mind.

FRAZER: Oh, all right – what brings you up to the Royal Hospital, doctor? Or is that a professional secret?

KILLICK: (*Smiling*) Oh, no – not at all. Gareth – my brother-in-law – was in a motor accident yesterday. He got away with a broken leg, but I promised my sister that I'd come down and see that they were looking after Gareth all right.

FRAZER: Where was the accident?

KILLICK: In Baker Street, actually. Why do you ask?

FRAZER: Well – it's just a coincidence, but a friend of mine was involved in a car smash yesterday.

KILLICK: Oh, I'm sorry to hear that. Was he badly hurt?

FRAZER: She, actually. A woman called Ruth Edwards. She's still on the danger list.

KILLICK: How did the accident happen?

FRAZER: I don't really know. Quite by chance I happened to pass by just after the accident occurred.

KILLICK: You saw her?

FRAZER: Yes. I travelled to the hospital with her in the ambulance. She's only a casual acquaintance really. I happened to find her spectacles one day and returned them to her.

KILLICK: Oh, I see. Well, I do hope she makes a quick recovery.

FRAZER: Thank you, doctor. And I hope your brother-in-law does the same.

KILLICK: Gareth? Oh, he'll be all right. Strong as an ox. Nevertheless, I'd better go round and see what they're doing to him. Keep my sister happy! You know what women are!

FRAZER: (*Smiling*) I do indeed.

FRAZER and KILLICK go out into the hall.

CUT TO: The Hall of FRAZER's Flat. Day.

FRAZER is opening the front door.

FRAZER: Thank you for delivering the letter. Most thoughtful.

KILLICK: Not at all. (*Offering his hand*) I didn't know whether it was important or not. Anyway, I thought it would save time.

FRAZER: (*Shakings hands*) It was very kind of you. Thanks for calling.

KILLICK goes out and FRAZER closes the door behind him and returns to the drawing room.

CUT TO: FRAZER's Drawing room. Day.

FRAZER enters and takes the letter from his pocket and reads it again. After a moment he slowly crosses to the telephone and dials a number. The voice of HOBSON is heard at the other end of the line.

HOBSON: Hello?

FRAZER: This is Tim Frazer. Can I speak to Mr Ross, please?

HOBSON: I'll see. One moment, sir.

A few moments later CHARLES ROSS comes on the phone. He is sitting in his office. For the duration of this conversation we cut back and forth between ROSS and FRAZER.

ROSS: Ross speaking. What is it, Frazer?

FRAZER: I want some information about a woman called Ma Dodsworth. She has a transport café on the road out of Broxbourne.

ROSS: What do you want to know? Anything in particular?

FRAZER: I'm going to see her, and I'd like to know a little about her.

ROSS: All right, I'll ring you back.

FRAZER: Another thing – I'd like to know whether a man was involved in a motor car accident yesterday and taken to the Royal Hospital.

ROSS: Do you know his name?

FRAZER: Only his Christian name – Gareth.

ROSS: Anything else?

FRAZER: No, but I'd like to see you sometime. Is that possible?

ROSS: Yes. We'll talk about that when I've got this information for you. Goodbye, Frazer.

FRAZER: Goodbye.

FRAZER replaces the telephone receiver.

The doorbell rings.

FRAZER goes out into the hall.

CUT TO: The Hall of FRAZER's Flat. Day.

FRAZER opens the front door. DONALD EDWARDS is there with a large parcel.

EDWARDS: Hello, Mr Frazer! I've returned the picture that you lent me.

FRAZER: Oh, come in, Mr Edwards! Do come in! You needn't have returned it just yet, Mr Edwards. You could have posted it to me later.

EDWARDS enters and FRAZER closes the front door.

EDWARDS: I didn't want it to get broken or anything.

FRAZER: Well, it's very kind of you. In here, please.

CUT TO: FRAZER's Drawing Room. Day.

FRAZER and DONALD EDWARDS enter.

FRAZER: Do sit down. I was terribly sorry about the accident. Have you been to the hospital this morning?

EDWARDS: (*Nodding*) There's still no change, I'm afraid.

FRAZER: Yes. I telephoned myself about an hour ago.

EDWARDS: It was really very good of you to take all that trouble yesterday. Going to the hospital with Ruth, and so on.

FRAZER: I could hardly have done less in the circumstances. But if there is anything else I can do ...?

EDWARDS: I'm worried, Mr Frazer – very worried. I've spent the best part of the morning at the police station.

FRAZER: The police station?

EDWARDS: They're not satisfied about the accident. They think the car had been tampered with.

FRAZER: Why on earth should they think that?

EDWARDS: I really don't know. The police are frightfully cagey, you know. They give very little away.

	I've told them, it's an absurd suggestion. Who on earth would tamper with Ruth's car?
FRAZER:	Well – what do you think happened?
EDWARDS:	It's hard to say, I must admit. Ruth was never a very good driver; slap-dash, you know. But the thing that puzzles me is – where was she going in the car, Mr Frazer? She nearly always tells me about her appointments, but I haven't the slightest idea where she was going yesterday. Er – she didn't say anything to you in the ambulance?
FRAZER:	No – I'm afraid not. She was only just conscious at the time. She did mutter a few words, but I'm afraid I didn't catch what they were. Perhaps the doctor could help you?
EDWARDS:	No, I've already spoken to him. He says that he heard nothing.
FRAZER:	I see. Well – I'm sorry I can't be more help. (*Suddenly*) Let me get you a drink! I'm sure you'd like a glass of sherry?
EDWARDS:	No – no, thank you, Mr Frazer. I didn't have any breakfast this morning, so I'd rather not, if you don't mind.
FRAZER:	Well, let me get you some breakfast. I'm not a bad cook.
EDWARDS:	No, no, really …
FRAZER:	Some coffee, then? That's ready.
EDWARDS:	No, thank you, Mr Frazer. I'd rather not, if you don't mind. I just wanted to bring the print back and thank you for yesterday.
FRAZER:	(*With a little nod*) It was quite a coincidence, yesterday, wasn't it? My turning up like that, I mean.

EDWARDS: Yes, yes it was, indeed. As a matter of fact, when the doctor told me I assumed you were on your way down to see us; perhaps to collect your friends' picture? (*He nods towards the parcel*)

FRAZER: (*Smiling*) No, actually, I was on my way to Farnham to see an old girl friend of mine.

EDWARDS: Oh, I see. Well – I must be going now. And thank you again, Mr Frazer, for being so kind.

FRAZER: Not at all. Let me show you out.

CUT TO: The Hall of FRAZER's Flat. Day.

FRAZER: By the way, does Anya know about her aunt?

EDWARDS: I had to tell her something, of course, but she doesn't know how serious it is.

FRAZER: What does the hospital say? When I phoned they merely said that she was on the danger list.

EDWARDS: Yes, well apparently the next twenty-four hours will tell. The skull is fractured, I believe.

FRAZER: If there's anything I can do, Mr Edwards, in any way at all – please don't hesitate to get in touch with me.

EDWARDS: Thank you. You've been very kind – we both appreciate it.

CUT TO: Embankment. London. Later the same morning.

FRAZER is standing by Cleopatra's Needle on the Embankment. After a moment a large, chauffeur-driven car pulls up in front of him. FRAZER gets into the back of the car.

125

CUT TO: Inside the car.

FRAZER is sitting in the back of the car with CHARLES ROSS. The car is stationary.

ROSS: I think I've got you the information you need on Ma Dodsworth.

FRAZER: Good.

ROSS: First of all, she's never been married though most people seem to call her Mrs Dodsworth. I don't quite know why.

FRAZER: Uh-huh.

ROSS: Apparently she's got quite a reputation – particularly in her own neighbourhood.

FRAZER: Good, bad, or indifferent?

ROSS: (*Smiling*) She's a bit of a mixture, really. A tough egg with a heart of gold.

FRAZER: I know exactly what you mean. She was poor but she was honest.

ROSS: (*Laughing*) Yes. Anyway, she manages to keep on the right side of the law.

FRAZER: What about the café? What's the business like?

ROSS: Not good, not bad. She makes a living. But why are you interested in this Ma Dodsworth?

FRAZER: Oh, I bumped into her once, and I thought I'd like to know a little more about her.

ROSS: (*Looking at FRAZER*) I see. The other thing you asked about – the accident at the Royal Hospital –

FRAZER: Yes?

ROSS: We checked on it. A man named Gareth Humphreys was admitted yesterday at four o'clock. He'd been in a car smash in Baker Street; he's got a broken leg. (*After a moment*) Anything else you want to know?

FRAZER: Yes, there is one more thing.

ROSS: Well?

FRAZER: How far will you back me, Ross, if I happen to get into trouble?

ROSS: With the police, you mean?

FRAZER: Perhaps.

ROSS: If you find Harry Denston for us we'll back you to the limit. That's a nice generalisation.

FRAZER: What's the limit?

ROSS: (*A moment: thoughtfully, looking at FRAZER*) The limit's murder – but of course we'd like you to have a very good reason for it. (*With the suggestion of a smile*) Preferably, self-defence.

FRAZER: (*Opening the car door*) I'll see what I can do.

ROSS: What have you got in mind, exactly?

FRAZER: (*Turning back to ROSS: seriously*) Someone's been taking me for a ride, and I don't like it! I'll find Denston for you and I'll find him within forty-eight hours!

FRAZER gets out of the car door and closes the door. ROSS looks after him.

CUT TO: MA's Place. Day.

MA DODSWORTH is busy behind the counter washing up. FRAZER enters, closing the door behind him, and crosses to the bar.

FRAZER: A cup of tea, please.

MA: (*Not looking up*) Righto, dear.

FRAZER goes to a table by the wall and sits down.

There is only one other CUSTOMER in the café and he has just finished his meal. After a moment he gets up and goes to the counter.

127

CUSTOMER: Box 'o matches, please, Ma.

MA: (*Straightening up*) Righto, luv.

MA turns and gets the matches from a shelf behind her. As she turns back again she sees FRAZER for the first time. She stops in mid-action, staring at him.

FRAZER looks up at her and she hurriedly goes on serving the CUSTOMER. She gives him the matches and takes his money. As she rings up the money on the till, she darts another glance at FRAZER. She gives the change to the CUSTOMER and he goes out.

MA pours a cup of tea and takes it over to FRAZER.

FRAZER: Sit down, Ma. I want to talk to you.

MA: I've got too much to do to sit and gossip, love.

FRAZER: (*As MA turns away*) I said – sit down, Ma.

MA: (*Turning: a shade angry*) Don't you talk like that to me, dear! I don't like being ordered about, you know.

FRAZER: You remember me, don't you, Ma?

MA: You been in here before, then?

FRAZER: Yes, I've been in here before. Do you know who I am?

MA: (*Smiling*) No, I don't dear. (*The smile fades*) And I couldn't care less. That'll be fourpence.

FRAZER: (*Feeling in his pockets*) My name's Phillips.

MA: That's nice. Fourpence, dearie – if you've got it.

FRAZER: (*Still feeling in his pockets*) Oh, I expect I'll manage it somehow. The pay at Scotland Yard isn't good – but it's not that bad.

MA: Scotland Yard? Who d'yer think yer kidding?

FRAZER: Don't you think I'm from the Yard?

MA:	No, I don't …
FRAZER:	All right, I show you my card. Phillips is the name. Detective Inspector Walter Hubert Phillips. Sorry about the Hubert, Ma.

FRAZER takes out his wallet, opens it and displays a card.
MA DODSWORTH doesn't look at it, instead she sits at the table.

MA:	Look, what do you want? You got nothing against me …
FRAZER:	(*Quite friendly*) I'm just making a few enquiries. Nothing to do with the local police – in fact, they needn't know anything about it, unless you want them to. (*Leaning forward, across the table*) I think you can help me, Ma.
MA:	I've never been mixed up in anything.
FRAZER:	Haven't you? Then you've been very lucky. Unless, of course, you've got an influential boyfriend.
MA:	(*With a grin: affably*) Why not get to the point, love. I haven't got all day, you know.
FRAZER:	All right, we'll get to the point. You remember when I was here last I asked you about a man and a woman; you said you'd seen them.

MA nods.

FRAZER:	You told me they'd been here the previous Friday.
MA:	That's right, love.

FRAZER takes his wallet out of his pocket and extracts a photograph from it. He pushes it across the table to MA.
It is a holiday snapshot showing HELEN BAKER and HARRY DENSTON, and FRAZER.

FRAZER points to HELEN and HARRY DENSTON in the picture.

FRAZER: Have you ever seen these two people before?

MA looks at the photograph, then at FRAZER.

MA: (*Shaking her head*) No, never see them before in me life. No. No!

FRAZER: But that's the girl, and the man, I spoke to you about. You described the girl very well. You said they'd been here – that you'd seen them.

MA: Yes, I know I did, love.

FRAZER: Well, why did you say that, if it wasn't true?

MA: Well, it's difficult to explain. You see … (*She hesitates*)

FRAZER: Did someone tell you to say it?

MA: (*After a moment*) Yes.

FRAZER: Who?

MA: Oh, just a pal of mine.

FRAZER: How much did this pal of yours pay you?

MA: Now don't be insulting, love. I did it as a favour. You don't think I'd take money from a pal of mine?

FRAZER: How much?

MA: Well – (*Looking at FRAZER*) – if you must know, I made a fiver out of it, and that's all. Honest, love – a fiver – not a bob more.

FRAZER: (*Smiling*) All right, I believe you. But I think you'd better tell me the whole story, don't you?

MA: (*After a little nod*) Well – this chap Tupper, him as has the garage down the road …

FRAZER: Tupper?

MA: Oh, you know the gent, do you, dear?

130

FRAZER:	We've met.
MA:	Yes, well, I can't say I'm surprised. Mind you, poor old Tupper's not really a crook, you know. Although, according to all accounts, some of his cars are a bit on the ropy side.
FRAZER:	Never mind the cars, what about Tupper?
MA:	Well – like I was saying – he comes up here one day last week and he has a cup of tea.
FRAZER:	Yes?
MA:	We got talking, like: and he asks me if I'd like to earn an easy fiver.
FRAZER:	And after careful deliberation you said, yes. Go on …
MA:	Well, he gave me a description of you and said you'd be calling in the caff and making enquiries about a young woman and her boy friend. I was to tell you that they'd both been here last Friday and that the gent was always popping in and out – one of my regulars, as you might say.
FRAZER:	Then what?
MA:	Then I was to phone Tupper and tell him you was here. And that's all – that's all I did.
FRAZER:	What about this other man – Lester? Had you ever seen him before?
MA:	No, dear, never clapped eyes on him. I was very surprised when he came in. I thought it'd be Tupper, as'd come, being as it was him oo'd arranged it all.
FRAZER:	Have you seen Tupper since I was here last?
MA:	Yes, he come in here the same afternoon. I asked him then who this fancy boy Lester

131

	was, and he said he was another car dealer. Tupper said they were trying to buy a car off you, but you wouldn't part.
FRAZER:	And you believed him?
MA:	Well, I dunno. I thought it sounded a bit off. I thought perhaps the three of you might be mixed up in some monkey business, you know – stolen cars, that sort of racket.
FRAZER:	I see. (*He looks at MA*)
MA:	(*A shade self-conscious*) I've told you the truth, dearie. I don't believe in getting on the wrong side of you boys.

FRAZER looks at MA for a moment, then suddenly rises from the table.

FRAZER:	Yes, alright, Ma. (*He turns towards the door and then hesitates*) Oh, I haven't paid for the tea.
MA:	That's all right, love. Have that one on the staff!

FRAZER gives MA a nod and goes out. MA stands looking towards the door.

CUT TO: Outside TUPPER's Garage. Day.

TUPPER has just finished serving a CUSTOMER who drives away as FRAZER drives up to the pumps in a brand new Jaguar. He speaks to TUPPER through the car window.

FRAZER:	Hello, Tupper! Can I have five gallons, please?
TUPPER:	Well – if it isn't Mr Frazer! Didn't recognise you for a minute.

FRAZER gets out of the car and stands watching TUPPER as he fills the tank.

TUPPER:	Nice little job you've got there.

FRAZER: Yes – it's not bad, is it? Only bought it yesterday, as a matter of fact.

TUPPER: New?

FRAZER: It's done about five thousand, that's all.

TUPPER: How much they rush you for that?

FRAZER: Just over eleven hundred.

TUPPER: (*Impressed*) Go on?

FRAZER: Was that cheap?

TUPPER: I should say so! That's a ruddy bargain, that is!

FRAZER: I bought it from a friend of mine – her husband's just died. Matter of fact, she had two cars there. I'm not so sure the other one wasn't a better bargain than this. (*With a shrug*) But I'm not up in the car racket.

TUPPER: What was it?

FRAZER: A Rover – '58, I think. Beautiful condition.

TUPPER nods: he looks at the Jaguar.

TUPPER: Well, this one's certainly a snip.

TUPPER puts the petrol pump back on its hook. FRAZER takes out his wallet and pays him for the petrol.

TUPPER: Thank you, Mr Frazer.

FRAZER opens the car door and gets in. TUPPER comes to the window.

TUPPER: (*After a moment*) About that other car – is it still for sale, d'yer know?

FRAZER: I think so, yes.

TUPPER: Do you think I could have a look at it?

FRAZER: Well – I told you, her husband's just died. It might be a little awkward, you know how it is.

TUPPER: Don't worry, I'd be tactful, if that's what you're thinkin'.

133

FRAZER: Yes, but she's rather a sensitive person, I
               wouldn't like her to think that … (*He
               hesitates*) I'll tell you what, Tupper. You
               come to my place tonight and we'll pop
               round together and have a look at it. She'll
               probably be all right about it, if I'm with
               you.

TUPPER: (*Pleased*) Yes, all right, sir. Ta. I'll do that.

FRASER takes his card from his pocket.

FRAZER: Here's my address.

TUPPER: Rightio! I'll be there about eight o'clock.

FRAZER: (*Nodding*) That'll do nicely.

*FRAZER, with a friendly nod to TUPPER, starts the car
engine and drives off.*

CUT TO: FRAZER's Drawing Room. Night.

*FRAZER is pouring a drink for TUPPER who is sitting in an
armchair watching him. He looks faintly disconsolate.*

FRAZER: Well, I'm sorry you had the journey for
               nothing, Mr Tupper! If only you could have
               got here a little earlier!

TUPPER: I know, mate. I tried, but I got held up at the
               garage till about half past nine.

FRAZER: Yes, I telephoned but there was no reply.
               Must have just missed you, I suppose.

TUPPER: You say, this bloke bought it this evening?

FRAZER: Yes, he gave her seven hundred for it. It <u>was</u>
               a '58. He was a dealer, I gather.

TUPPER: (*Disgusted*) Aah! Might have known it!
               These dealers! He'll make two hundred quid
               on that! Two hundred at least!

FRAZER: Yes, well – there you are. I'm sorry. Would
               you like another drink?

TUPPER: (*Rising*) No, thanks, ta. I'd better get back.

134

FRAZER:	(*Casually*) Of course, if it's just a question of two hundred pounds, I know how you could make it – just like that. (*He snaps his fingers*)
TUPPER:	(*Interested*) Go on – how?
FRAZER:	By telling me what happened to that car I sold you, the Hillman Minx.
TUPPER:	Thanks for the drink. I must be getting along now.
FRAZER:	Doesn't two hundred pounds interest you, then?
TUPPER:	Oh, sure, it interests me. I'm a sucker for easy money. But I'm sorry, chum. (*He shakes his head*) I'm not talking about that particular car.
FRAZER:	All right, Tupper, I'll make you another proposition.

TUPPER looks at FRAZER guardedly.

FRAZER:	I met a man called Lester at Ma's place. He came to see me in answer to a phone call that Ma Dodsworth made to you.
TUPPER:	I don't know anything about this! I dunno what you're talking about, chum!
FRAZER:	I think you do, Tupper. But what interests me is this: it took Lester over an hour to get to the café after Ma telephoned you.
TUPPER:	Well?
FRAZER:	So Lester couldn't have been waiting at the garage – your place is only five minutes from the café.
TUPPER:	I just don't know what the hell you're talking about!
FRAZER:	Don't you? Then I'll tell you. As soon as you heard from Ma Dodsworth you

telephoned Lester. It took him just over an hour to get to Ma's Place.

TUPPER: (*Angrily*) You're nuts! I've never even heard of anyone called Lester.

TUPPER moves towards the hall.

FRAZER: I'll give you two hundred pounds, Tupper – if you'll tell me the number you called.

TUPPER stops dead: turns and looks at FRAZER.

There is a pause.

TUPPER: Two hundred quid?

FRAZER: Yes.

TUPPER: Just for the phone number?

FRAZER: That's right.

TUPPER: Have you got the two hundred quid – here, I mean?

FRAZER crosses to his desk, opens a drawer, and takes out a bundle of five pound notes.

TUPPER looks at them, then at FRAZER.

TUPPER: (*Moving towards the drinks table: nervously*) Let's get this straight. All you want is the phone number?

FRAZER: (*Nodding*) As soon as you heard from Ma Dodsworth you telephoned Lester. I want that phone number – nothing else.

TUPPER hesitates, looks at the money again.

TUPPER: It was Kensington 7255.

There is a tiny pause, then FRAZER nods.

FRAZER: All right, Tupper.

TUPPER picks up the notes and puts them in his pocket.

TUPPER: (*Tensely*) Now remember – if you're ever asked, I never gave you that number, I never even seen you tonight. You understand?

FRAZER: (*Quietly*) Yes, I understand.

TUPPER goes out into the hall. We hear the front door open and close.

FRAZER lights a cigarette. He wanders to the telephone and stands for a moment, staring down at it. Then suddenly he picks up the receiver and dials the number. We hear the number ringing out at the other end, followed by HELEN's voice.

HELEN: Kensington 7255.

FRAZER: (*After a momentary pause*) This is Tim. I wondered if you'd like to have lunch with me tomorrow, Helen?

CUT TO: Outside TUPPER's Garage. Day.

TUPPER is just finishing serving a MOTOR-CYCLIST, who is muffled up in crash helmet, leather jacket, goggles, etc. The MOTOR-CYCLIST gives TUPPER some money and TUPPER goes into the office to get change. At that moment a car drives up on the opposite side of the road. It stops and LESTER gets out. He stands, hands in pockets, looking across to the garage as the car drives on again. He comes across towards the garage.

TUPPER comes out of the office and gives the MOTOR-CYCLIST his change. The MOTOR-CYCLIST stands buttoning his jacket as if in readiness to continue his journey.

TUPPER looks up and sees LESTER. He stands petrified for a moment, then decides to brazen it out and crosses to LESTER, smiling nervously.

TUPPER: Hello, Mr Lester! Fancy seeing you here!

LESTER: You know how I like to keep in touch with old friends, Tupper.

TUPPER: That's right.

LESTER: I've been hearing some stories about you,
             Tupper. (*He smiles*) You've been a naughty
             boy, haven't you?

TUPPER tries to smile back.

TUPPER: I don't know what you mean, Mr Lester.

LESTER: Someone told me you went to London last
             night.

TUPPER: That's right, Mr Lester: had a deal on, I did.
             That's right.

LESTER: Go on? I heard different. I heard you went
             to see Frazer.

TUPPER: Ah, now, you're right, Mr Lester! You're
             dead right, son. There ain't much that gets
             past you, I can see that! He had a friend,
             see? And this friend of his – she had a car
             she wanted to sell, see? So when I went up
             there …

TUPPER's voice trails off under LESTER's rigid smile.

LESTER: You've been talking to Frazer, haven't you?

TUPPER: (*Panicky*) No! No, I haven't! Like I said – it
             was about a car, see?

LESTER: About a car?

TUPPER: Yes, that's right, guv …

LESTER: What car? The Hillman?

TUPPER: No, 'course not! I never said a word about
             the Hillman. Honest, I didn't, Lester!

LESTER: (*After a moment: quietly, looking at
             TUPPER*) You know, you really ought to be
             more careful who you deal with, Tupper.

TUPPER: Oh, I will in future, Mr Lester! I will, Mr
             Lester, straight up, I will!

*LESTER turns to the MOTOR-CYCLIST, who is still
standing astride his machine and nods.*

The MOTOR-CYCLIST starts his engine and revs it up to full pitch.

TUPPER, scared, looks at the MOTOR-CYCLIST and then at LESTER. He sees that LESTER now has a revolver in his hand. LESTER is smiling at him.

TUPPER stretches out a hand as if to ward off the bullets. Covered by the noise of the motor bike, LESTER shoots TUPPER in the stomach.

TUPPER reels back against the wall of the office, clutching his stomach and then sinks to the ground.

LESTER crosses, gets on the pillion of the motor cycle, and the two men drive off.

CUT TO: FRAZER's Drawing Room. Day.

HELEN is sitting in an armchair. FRAZER is standing pouring drinks from a cocktail shaker.

HELEN: You oughtn't to keep plying me with drinks, Tim. I'm feeling quite tiddly already.

FRAZER: Nonsense! It'll do you good to relax for once.

HELEN: Well – it's lucky I haven't got a matinee today, that's all.

FRAZER: (*Smiling*) Well, it's come to a pretty pass if you can't have a farewell drink with a friend!

HELEN: Farewell drink! Darling, I've had four of these Martinis already!

FRAZER laughs.

HELEN: Tim, why have you suddenly decided to go abroad like this?

FRAZER: It's not really sudden – I've been thinking about it for some time. Now I've got the money from Harry, there's really nothing to keep me here any longer.

HELEN: Yes, well, it's all rather sad, darling.

139

FRAZER: (*A shrug*) If dear old Harry wants to cut himself off from his old friends – that's his affair. Here, read the letter he sent me.

FRAZER takes the letter from his pocket and hands it to HELEN.

She reads it while FRAZER stands watching her. HELEN finishes the letter and hands it back to FRAZER.

HELEN: It seems pretty final, doesn't it?

FRAZER: (*Nodding*) Yes, not exactly brimming over with bonhomie! But what about you, Helen – and the engagement? (*Tapping the letter*) Are you included in this fond farewell?

HELEN: (*After a pause*) That time I saw him I tried to discuss our engagement and everything. He just wasn't interested. Well, he's not the only fish in the sea, I suppose.

FRAZER: No, but unfortunately you don't forget people like Harry Denston, you don't just brush them out of your life; it's not as easy as all that.

HELEN: I know …

FRAZER: (*Suddenly: looking at HELEN*) Well, so what happened, Helen – when you met him, the other night?

HELEN: (*Surprised and embarrassed by the question*) But I've already told you all there is to know – there's nothing more.

FRAZER: Yes, but the thing that puzzles me is why Harry should have chosen a café like that for your meeting.

HELEN looks at FRAZER: she is curious.

FRAZER nods.

FRAZER: Yes, I went there. It's a real dump, isn't it? The juke-box blaring out all the time, I wonder you could hear yourself speak!

HELEN: (*Evasively: turning away*) You know Harry. He always liked noisy places.

FRAZER: Yes, but I shouldn't have thought he'd have liked Ma Dodsworth's.

HELEN: (*Looking at her watch*) Tim, would you mind terribly if we didn't lunch together today? I think I've got one of my headaches coming on, and that always means …

HELEN starts rising from the armchair.

FRAZER: (*Stopping HELEN*) Helen, I've always thought you were a very good actress. (*Looking at HELEN*) But I never realised, until just recently, what a very good liar you are as well.

HELEN stares at FRAZER in surprise, then does rise from the armchair.

HELEN: What on earth do you mean by that?

FRAZER: There's no juke-box in Ma Dodsworht's café, there's no music of any kind. (*He takes hold of HELEN's arm*) You've never been to the place! Have you, Helen?

HELEN: I don't know what you're talking about!

FRAZER: Your whole story was a pack of lies! You didn't go to the café – you didn't see Harry.

HELEN: (*A shade frightened*) What do you mean? I don't know what you mean?

FRAZER: I think you do! You told me that story about Harry because you knew that as soon as I'd heard it I'd go to the café. Well, I went, Helen! I went and I met your charming little friend Lester.

HELEN: Tim, I swear …

FRAZER: I don't care what you say. (*Shaking his head*) I don't know how you fit into all this, Helen, but by God I'm going to find out!

141

| HELEN: | (*Feeling her head*) I've got a dreadful headache and you're just talking a lot of nonsense, so please let me … |

HELEN makes a move towards the hall. FRAZER grabs her arm.

FRAZER:	Listen to me! Whatever it is you're mixed up in, murder's only a small part of it.
HELEN:	(*Shocked: interrupting TIM*) Murder?
FRAZER:	Yes, murder! Tupper's dead. He was shot in the stomach. He died this morning.
HELEN:	(*Dazed: shaking her head*) But I don't know anyone called Tupper! I don't know what you're talking about …
FRAZER:	(*Tensely: angry*) Oh, yes, you do – and it's not the only thing you know!
HELEN:	… You're hurting my arm!
FRAZER:	… You've taken me for a ride long enough, Helen! You know where Harry is, and you're going to tell me! Because if you don't …
HELEN:	Tim, please! My arm …
FRAZER:	I want the truth, Helen! Where's Harry?
HELEN:	I don't – know where he is …
FRAZER:	The truth, Helen – where is Harry?
HELEN:	All right … all right – he's at Henton.
FRAZER:	At Henton? I don't believe you!
HELEN:	He is! He is, I tell you! He's been there the whole time!

HELEN bursts into tears. FRAZER stands and looks at her as if trying to weigh up the truth of her statement.

End of Episode Five

Episode Six

OPEN TO: FRAZER's Drawing Room. Day.

A tense, dejected looking HELEN is sitting on the settee.
FRAZER is standing, looking down at her.

HELEN: (*Tensely*) I'm telling you the truth, Tim! Harry's in Henton!

FRAZER: Where exactly in Henton?

HELEN: (*Shaking her head*) I don't know. I just know he's in Henton, that's all. (*She looks up at FRAZER*) It's the truth, if you don't believe me, well – (*A shrug*) – that's just too bad.

FRAZER: Helen, I'm sorry I had to get tough with you just now, but – I hadn't any choice.

HELEN: I'm not feeling too good. I'm going home.

FRAZER: (*Restraining HELEN, quietly*) I'm sorry, you can't do that. (*Looking at his watch*) I've got someone coming to see you at three o'clock.

HELEN looks at FRAZER, surprised.

FRAZER: We can go out and have some lunch, or you can – (*He nods towards the bedroom*) – have a rest in the bedroom, which ever you like.

HELEN: But I don't want to see anyone! I just don't feel like …

FRAZER: (*Interrupting HELEN*) I'm sorry. I'm afraid you've got to, Helen.

HELEN: Who are these people?

FRAZER: Some friends of mine.

HELEN: The police?

FRASER: (*Shaking his head*) No, not the police – exactly.

HELEN: Well, who are they?

FRAZER: (*Quietly, looking at his watch again*) Which is it to be, Helen? Would you like some lunch, or would you prefer …

HELEN: No, I wouldn't! I want to go home!

145

FRAZER: You can go home as soon as you've seen these friends of mine, I promise you … (*With the suggestion of a smile*) Helen, I don't want to have to get tough with you again!

HELEN: (*Picking up her fur stole off the armchair*) I'm not exactly crazy on the idea either. (*She crosses to the bedroom*) Let me know when your – friends arrive.

HELEN goes into the bedroom.

FRAZER gives a little sigh of relief: feels his brow, and then crosses to the drinks table.

CUT TO: FRAZER's Drawing Room. Day. An hour later.

CHARLES ROSS is sitting in the armchair in FRAZER's flat, thoughtfully putting a cigarette into his holder and looking towards HELEN who is sitting on the settee. FRAZER is standing by the drinks table.

ROSS: You say, this man Lester came to see you about a fortnight ago?

HELEN: Yes, I think it was a fortnight ago. I'm not sure of the date.

ROSS: Go on, Miss Baker.

HELEN: He called on me at the theatre. I'd never seen him before and I wondered what he wanted. He told me that my fiancé, Harry Denston, was in trouble – serious trouble. He said that Harry had stolen something and was likely to be arrested.

ROSS: Did he tell you what it was that your fiancé had stolen?

HELEN: No, he was terribly vague about it. In any case, I didn't believe him, it sounded nonsense to me.

FRAZER: Then what convinced you he was telling the truth?

HELEN: A telephone call from Harry.

146

FRAZER: From Harry?

HELEN: Yes. Lester said he'd arrange for Harry to speak to me. He called at my flat the next day and while he was there Harry telephoned.

FRAZER: Go on …

HELEN: Harry sounded desperate; he really frightened me. He said that if he was to come out of this alive, I must do everything that Lester told me to.

FRAZER: You're sure it was Harry?

HELEN: I'm positive. It was during this call that Harry let slip that he was at Henton. I think it was just a slip of the tongue, but Lester got furious. He said that if I told anyone where Harry was they'd hand him straight over to the police.

FRAZER: And what did Lester want you to do? Try to persuade me to forget Harry – to get off his trail, as it were?

HELEN: Yes – that was the main thing. He told me that he and his friends were trying to get Harry out of the country. The first thing I'd got to do was to pay Harry's debts for him …

FRAZER: So it was your money?

HELEN: Yes – I'm afraid so. The idea was that once you had the money you'd stop bothering about Harry. Anyway, I agreed to do this, and I did it.

ROSS: What else?

HELEN: I was to tell Tim that I'd met Harry at Ma Dodsworth's. I'd never been to the place, of course – that's where I slipped up, Lester hoped that Tim wouldn't go there – in which case he'd know for certain that he'd given up looking for Harry.

FRAZER: (*To ROSS*) But I did go, and I received a nice friendly warning from Mr Lester.

147

ROSS: He seems a bright boy, our Lester.

FRAZER: Oh, he is!

ROSS: (*To HELEN*) Is Lester the only contact you've had with these people?

HELEN: Yes. I've seen no-one else.

ROSS: And you've heard no suggestions as to who they might be?

HELEN: No – none at all, I'm afraid. (*After a moment*) I suppose I've just been a nuisance to everybody – but I was doing what seemed to be the only thing possible to save Harry. I know him so well. He's just the sort to get mixed up in a crooked business like this – and then be made the scapegoat!

FRAZER: How did he get mixed up in it? Do you know?

HELEN: Well, by stealing this … thing – I imagine.

FRAZER: And what about the model on my mantelpiece, Helen? You told me it was Harry that asked you to take the photograph. Was it?

HELEN: No – I'm afraid it wasn't. It was Lester. But I couldn't tell you that without telling you the whole story.

ROSS: He just told you to take a photograph of the model and send the film to the shop in Camden Town?

HELEN: Bonnington's – yes.

ROSS: Why?

HELEN: I don't know why. I honestly don't! (*She rises*) I know my story sounds a very unlikely one, and I know in many ways I've been stupid, but I've only …

ROSS: (*Interrupting HELEN*) You have. You have indeed been stupid, Miss Baker. Very stupid. (*He

148

rises and looks at HELEN) Nevertheless, I believe you.

HELEN: (With a look at FRAZER) Well that's something, anyway!

FRAZER: I wish you'd told us this earlier, Helen.

HELEN: I know. I should have done. But I was frightened of Lester and I just didn't know what might happen to Harry if I told anyone.

ROSS: (Nodding) You were in a difficult position, I can see that. But you should have confided in Mr Frazer, if you'd done that …

HELEN: Yes, but I didn't know what Tim was up to – or who he was working for! (Looking at ROSS) I still don't, if it comes to that!

ROSS gives a little smile and takes out his cigarette lighter.

ROSS: I understand your show comes off at the end of the week, Miss Baker?

HELEN: Yes, it does.

ROSS: D'you think you could get away before then?

HELEN: Get away?

ROSS: Yes – I'd like you to be out of the way during the next two or three days. Could you leave the show, now, today – fly over to Paris, perhaps?

HELEN: Well, I don't know. It certainly wouldn't be easy …

ROSS: Why? Haven't you got an understudy?

HELEN: Well, yes …

ROSS: Then give the poor girl a chance, Miss Baker.

HELEN: Are you serious about this?

ROSS: Quite serious. I think certain things are going to happen during the next two or three days. If something goes wrong – and it might, very easily – Lester might take it into his head to drop in on you. I shouldn't like that, Miss Baker. I don't think you would, either.

HELEN: But what about Harry?

ROSS: Don't you think you've given your fiancé sufficient thought, for the time being? In any case, you won't help him by staying here, I assure you.

FRAZER: I'll look after Harry, Helen.

HELEN: (*After a moment*) All right, Mr Ross. (*She holds out her hand to him*) Paris it is.

HELEN and ROSS shake hands.

HELEN: I'll be at the Meurice, if you want me.

HELEN goes into the hall with FRAZER. ROSS flicks the lighter and lights his cigarette. FRAZER returns.

FRAZER: Well – what do you make of it?

ROSS: She's telling the truth now; it's a pity she didn't before, of course.

FRAZER: (*Nodding*) Ross, is it true about Harry? Did he steal something?

ROSS looks at FRAZER, hesitates, then crosses and sits on the arm of the settee.

ROSS: Yes.

FRAZER: What was it?

ROSS: Have you ever heard of a man called John Sinclair White?

FRAZER: The name seems familiar.

ROSS: He's very well known in his own, rather specialised, field. He's a metallurgist. For years now he's been working on a new alloy – it became rather a joke in scientific circles – but at last he's perfected it.

FRAZER: What's so special about it?

150

ROSS: It's light, cheap to manufacture, almost as strong as steel and – most important of all – it's resistant to radio-activity.

FRAZER: To what extent?

ROSS: I'm a layman, Frazer – so I can only talk to you in layman's language. Apparently, a quarter inch thickness of this metal is equal to an eighteen inch thickness of lead.

FRAZER: But that's fantastic!

ROSS: Quite. So fantastic that a great many people, not always responsible people at that, became interested in it.

FRAZER: But how does Harry Denston fit into all this?

ROSS: I'm coming to that. Denston got to know White and tried to borrow money from him. White refused – they had a blazing row and that was, seemingly, the end of the matter.

FRAZER: Not if I know Harry!

ROSS: Quite. Anyway, a certain gentleman – let's call him X for the moment – scraped up an acquaintance with Harry and offered him a pretty large sum of money for a microfilm of White's formula.

FRAZER: Trading on the fact, of course, that Harry knew White and was still angry with him?

ROSS: Exactly. The idea appealed to Harry and he decided to have a shot at it. Well, he was lucky. He got the film, but having got it he decided …

FRAZER: That X hadn't offered him enough for it, and he was going to sell it on the open markct …

ROSS: (*Smiling*) You obviously know your friend! That's exactly what happened. However, to keep X happy, Harry prepared a second film, with a dud formula on it, and gave it to him.

151

FRAZER: Go on …

ROSS: Harry knew that X had been in touch with a group of East German officials and that he has also contacted an armaments combine in Western Germany. He was, in fact, playing one off against the other. Harry decided to do the same. The Eastern Germans told Harry to meet Anstrov, their representative, at Henton. They told Harry that Anstrov would pay the price he wanted and collect the film. But Harry was taking no chances. First of all, he let it be known that his reason for going to Henton was to meet you – this was in case X became suspicious – and secondly, he made up his mind not to take the film to Henton. Well, you know what happened.

FRAZER: No, I don't know what happened!

ROSS: Harry went to Henton – he arrived the day before you did – and stayed at the pub under the name of Hemingway. Suddenly, Mr Hemingway disappears – (*He snaps his fingers*) – just like that.

FRAZER: You mean he was kidnapped?

ROSS: Yes.

FRAZER: By whom?

ROSS: What's your guess, Frazer?

FRAZER: Well, obviously by one of the German groups or by X, who had found out that he was being double-crossed.

ROSS: Yes. (*He rises and moves across to the drinks table*) Anyway, whoever it is, it's quite obvious they haven't made him talk yet. According to our information he's still holding out.

FRAZER: Yes, Harry would.

152

ROSS: (*Turning, looking at FRAZER*) I'm glad to hear you say that.

FRAZER: Oh, don't underrate him. He's an irresponsible devil, and you couldn't trust him a yard with your wife or girlfriend – but he's got plenty of guts.

ROSS: And he'll need them, Frazer. May I help myself to a drink?

FRAZER: (*His thoughts still on HARRY DENSTON*) Yes, of course.

ROSS begins to mix himself a whisky and soda.

CUT TO: The Village Street, Henton. Early Evening.
FRAZER's car, the Jaguar, pulls up in front of The Three Bells. FRAZER gets out of the car, goes round to the boot, and takes out a suitcase.

CUT TO: Inside The Three Bells. Evening.
NORMAN and MADGE are busy serving customers. Among those at the bar we see PC MUIR, in uniform but off duty, and several fishermen. One of them, a small wiry man named WILL TRUMAN, is in the middle of telling a story.

WILL: … and there's this terrible row going on, so the Skipper says to me, "We'd best take a look at this, Will," so I says, "Righto," and we pulls alongside this cabin cruiser and I clambers aboard.

The door opens and FRAZER enters the bar, carrying his suitcase. He walks up to the bar, outside the group surrounding WILL TRUMAN. During the following scene we hear WILL TRUMAN's story in the background, punctuated by bursts of laughter from his audience.

MADGE: Hello, Mr Frazer! We got your telegram – nice surprise seeing you again so soon.

153

FRAZER: (*Looking around the bar*) It's nice to be
                 back.

NORMAN: I'll get young Billy to take your bag up.
                 You're in your old room, if that's all right?

FRAZER: That's fine.

NORMAN goes to the kitchen door and calls through.

NORMAN: Billy! Come and take Mr Frazer's bag up to
                 Number 8, will you?

NORMAN comes back to the bar.

*A customer calls him from the other end and he moves off to
serve him.*

*BILLY, a boy of about sixteen comes out of the kitchen, sees
FRAZER's bag and picks it up.*

BILLY: (*To MADGE*) This is the one?

MADGE: That's it, Billy. Number 8.

BILLY goes off up the staircase with the suitcase.

MADGE: Billy's my young cousin – we're looking
                 after him for a week or two.

FRAZER: I'll have a drink now I'm here, if I may. I
                 can't tempt you to have something with me,
                 I suppose?

MADGE: (*Pouring a drink*) You know me!

*While MADGE is busy FRAZER turns his attention to the
group round the bar. WILL TRUMAN is still holding his
audience.*

WILL: … And he pushes his great hairy face into
                 mine and he says, "If you don't take
                 yourself off my boat, I'll damn well string
                 you up!"

They all roar with laughter at this. FRAZER smiles.

WILL: No – wait! I haven't finished yet! He'd got
                 hold of me and he was breathing all over me
                 like a brewery – you could've lit his breath
                 with a match. Suddenly the Skipper comes

up and taps him on the shoulder and says, "You can't treat one o' my men like that," he says. So Old Rembrandt turns round to him, very slow like, and he grabs hold of the Skipper and says, "It don't matter about one of your men," he says, "one more squeak out of you, and I'll pitch you both in the hog-wash!"

The others roar with laughter again.

WILL: And he would, too!

FISHERMAN: Too right, he would! There's always a row coming from that boat. I just let well alone – pretend I don't hear nothing!

WILL: Best way! That's what I'll do in future. These artists – they're all up the wall!

MUIR: He sells a lot of his pictures up in London, mind.

WILL: He wouldn't sell 'em round here! People got more sense!

FRAZER has now got his drink and is leaning comfortably against the bar. PC MUIR turns and sees him.

MUIR: How are you, Mr Frazer? All right.

FRAZER: I'm fine, thanks. How are you keeping?

MUIR: Mustn't grumble, you know. Mustn't grumble.

FRAZER: Been having a bit of excitement round here?

MUIR: What, you mean old Will? No – nothing special – there's always something going on with that artist chap. (*Laughing*) Mad as a hatter!

FRAZER: What's his name – the artist?

MUIR: Well, his real name's Walters, but they all call him Rembrandt hereabouts – being as he's an artist, see?

FRAZER: Yes, I see.

FRAZER turns to put his glass down and as he does so he looks towards the staircase. His expression changes. DONALD EDWARDS comes down the staircase, carrying a suitcase.

FRAZER: (*To MUIR*) Excuse me a moment.

FRAZER crosses to the bottom of the staircase. EDWARDS looks up and sees FRAZER. He is obviously very surprised.

EDWARDS: Why, Mr Frazer! What on earth are you doing in this part of the world?

FRAZER: I often come up here – especially when I'm in need of a little peace and quiet. (*Smiling*) Although I don't always find it, I'm afraid!

EDWARDS: This is quite extraordinary! But when did you arrive?

FRAZER: About five minutes ago.

EDWARDS: Oh, dear, and I'm just leaving! What a pity …

BILLY comes down the staircase and takes EDWARDS' suitcase from him.

BILLY: I'll see if the taxi's here, Mr Edwards.

EDWARDS: Thank you. Thank you very much.

BILLY goes out of the main door into the street.

FRAZER: Have you been here long?

EDWARDS: No, no, I arrived last night. I had a telephone message from a customer of mine who lives down here; he's bought himself a yacht and he wants me to make a model of it. I told him I could do it from photographs, but he insisted on my coming down here. So stupid, really! Just a waste of time! (*Shaking his head*) I've still got to have the photographs.

FRAZER: Have you been down here before, then?

156

EDWARDS: Once, a very long time ago. It's a pleasant part of the country but a little too – er – rugged for my liking.

FRAZER: I know what you mean. (*Pleasantly*) How's Mrs Edwards?

EDWARDS: Oh, she's quite a lot better, thank goodness. The hospital appear quite pleased with her, in fact.

FRAZER: Good. Give her my best wishes when you see her.

EDWARDS: I will indeed. (*Glancing at the clock on the wall*) My goodness, I must fly – or I shall miss my train! What a pity you didn't arrive yesterday, Mr Frazer, we could have had dinner together.

BILLY returns from the street.

BILLY: (*To EDWARDS*) The car's here!

EDWARDS: (*Nodding*) Yes, all right. Billy. Well – er – goodbye, Mr Frazer.

FRAZER and EDWARDS shake hands.

FRAZER: Goodbye! Don't forget to give my regards to your wife.

EDWARDS: I won't.

EDWARDS goes out into the street, followed by BILLY. FRAZER stands for a moment, looking towards the door. Then he returns to the bar and picks up his drink.

CUT TO: Inside The Three Bells. Evening.

NORMAN is behind the bar pulling a pint for a customer who is standing at the bar. MADGE is going round clearing up glasses. FRAZER comes down the staircase and crosses to his usual corner.

MADGE: Like a drink before supper, Mr Frazer?

FRAZER:	No, thanks. I'd like a word with your father and yourself, though, if you can spare a moment?
MADGE:	(*Surprised*) Yes, of course. (*She calls*) Dad!
NORMAN:	(*Serving a customer; looking up*) Aye?
MADGE:	Could you come over a minute?

NORMAN takes the customer's money and rings it up on the till, having done this he crosses to MADGE and FRAZER. He sits on the other side of the table.

NORMAN:	You want me, Mr Frazer?
FRAZER:	You remember the first time I was here, I was due to meet a friend of mine called Harry Denston?
NORMAN:	Aye, that's right – never turned up.
MADGE:	But he phoned you last time you were here. I thought you were going to meet him in London?
FRAZER:	Yes, I was. But he didn't show up in London, either. (*To NORMAN*) Anyway, I've got a photograph of Harry Denston and I'd like you and Madge to take a look at it.

FRAZER takes several photographs from his pocket and spreads them out on the table. MADGE and NORMAN look at the photographs.

MADGE:	(*Suddenly*) But this is Mr Hemingway!
NORMAN:	That's right – Mr Hemingway!

MADGE and NORMAN look at FRAZER.

FRAZER:	(*Quietly*) Tell me about Mr Hemingway, Norman.
NORMAN:	Well, it was about the time of the big storm. (*Pointing to the photograph*) This fellow Hemingway booked in here – said he'd be staying a few days.
MADGE:	He didn't, though.

NORMAN: He did not! Booked in on a Tuesday, I think it was. Next morning he'd vamoosed – gone.

FRAZER: Just like that?

NORMAN: Just like that! Went up to his room on the Tuesday night and that was the last we ever saw of him. Bed wasn't slept in nor nothing.

FRAZER: I see.

MADGE: We thought he'd done a flit, like – so's not to pay his bill, but next day, so far as I remember …

NORMAN: Aye – the very next day.

MADGE: …We got a letter from him saying he'd had to leave sudden like. He enclosed a five-pound note.

NORMAN: To cover his bill, like. Very generous, I must say.

FRAZER: I suppose you wouldn't still have the letter?

NORMAN: Have we got that letter, Madge?

MADGE: Aye – I think we have. I put it in that box under the counter. I'll see if it's there still.

MADGE goes across to the bar.

FRAZER: And you've never seen this Mr Hemingway since?

NORMAN: No, not a sign. You say it's your friend Denston, do you?

FRAZER: (*Indicating photographs*) Well – this is Harry Denston.

NORMAN: And that's Mr Hemingway! So it must be the same bloke. (*Marvelling*) Well, you never can tell, can you?

MADGE returns to them, the letter in her hand.

MADGE: Here we are – I knew I'd kept it somewhere.

FRAZER: D'you mind if I read it?

159

NORMAN: Go ahead.

FRAZER takes the letter and glances through it. While he is doing so DR KILLICK enters from the street. He sees the group round the bench and comes over to them.

KILLICK: Well, Mr Frazer! Good evening!

FRAZER: Hello, doctor! (*About to rise*) How are you?

KILLICK: No, don't get up. Fine, thank you, fine! What brings you to this part of the world?

FRAZER: Sit down, doctor. Perhaps you can shed some light on this mystery.

KILLICK: (*Sitting down*) Mystery? What mystery? Don't tell me Madge has been watering the beer again!

MADGE: (*Laughing*) Now, Dr Killick, please!

NORMAN laughs.

FRAZER: (*To KILLICK*) This letter is from a Mr Hemingway who stayed here – or rather booked a room – about three weeks ago.

NORMAN: Just about the time when we 'ad that bad storm, doctor!

FRAZER: (*Nodding*) That's right. Mr Hemingway arrived and was shown to his room. Next morning he'd disappeared – gone. Twenty-four hours later Norman received this letter with a five-pound note.

KILLICK: (*Taking the letter*) Well, that was pretty generous. (*He reads the letter*) This letter says he had to leave suddenly, on business.

FRAZER: Yes.

KILLICK: Well, what's wrong with that?

FRAZER: Two things, doctor. First of all – the mysterious Mr Hemingway happens to be my ex-business partner, Harry Denston. (*He*

160

	points to the photographs) Norman and Madge have identified him.
KILLICK:	(*Surprised*) Oh ...
FRAZER:	And secondly, this letter wasn't written by Mr Hemingway, alias Harry Denston.
NORMAN:	(*Surprised*) It wasn't?
FRAZER:	No.
MADGE:	How do you know that?
FRAZER:	(*Tapping the photographs*) Because I know Harry's handwriting. I know it as well as I know my own.
MADGE:	Well, perhaps someone wrote the letter for him – maybe he was busy. He must have been pretty busy to dash off like that.
FRAZER:	Yes – or maybe he didn't know anything about the letter.
KILLICK:	I don't quite follow you, Mr Frazer?
FRAZER:	Look at it this way; suppose Denston didn't want to leave here, but was kidnapped ...
MADGE:	Kidnapped!
NORMAN:	Good gracious, Mr Frazer!
KILLICK:	Surely that's a bit far-fetched, my dear fellow?
FRAZER:	Is it far-fetched, doctor? (*Shaking his head*) I don't think so. It fits the facts. Suddenly, in the middle of the night, this man disappears. Twenty-four hours later Norman receives a letter – supposedly sent by Hemingway – explaining why he disappeared so suddenly. Naturally, Norman's perfectly satisfied now – not a bit curious. Why should he be? He's made a fiver out of it, anyway.

161

KILLICK: Yes, it sounds quite logical, but – really, Mr Frazer, kidnapping! (*Smiling*) I think you're jumping to conclusions. (*A sudden thought*) Unless, of course, you've a specific reason for believing that your friend was kidnapped?

FRAZER: No. (*Also smiling*) No, I haven't a specific reason, doctor.

NORMAN: Still, it's rum. There's no getting away from that. Whichever way you look at it, it's very rum.

KILLICK: Madge, I've come to ask you a favour.

MADGE: Yes, of course, doctor. What is it?

KILLICK: Miss Hoskins has broken her leg …

MADGE: Oh, the poor thing! When did this happen?

KILLICK: About an hour ago. She slipped on the stairs and fell down the whole flight.

NORMAN: Oh, dear – that's not going to do her much good at her time of life!

KILLICK: No. (*To MADGE*) Anyway, I've phoned for an ambulance, but I've got to go out on another call, so I wonder if you could pop round and sit with her for a little while? She's only got her sister with her at the moment, and she's not much help.

MADGE: 'Course I will, doctor. I'll just run and put my coat on.

KILLICK: She's quite comfortable – but just keep her company for a bit.

MADGE goes off into the kitchen.

NORMAN: Would you like a drink, doctor?

KILLICK: No, thank you, Norman. I must be on my way! Good night, Mr Frazer. I hope I'll see you again before you go back to London.

162

FRAZER: I hope so, doctor. I'll be around …

KILLICK goes out into the street. MADGE comes out of the kitchen and follows him, calling to NORMAN as she does so.

MADGE: Won't be long, dad!

FRAZER: You're not very busy tonight, Norman?

NORMAN: We shall be in a few minutes – they're all over at the big darts match at the Crown. My regulars will be back as soon as it's over.

FRAZER: Nice chap – Dr Killick.

NORMAN: Oh, aye – very popular in Henton, is Dr Killick. And we don't take much to strangers in these parts, not when they settle down here.

FRAZER: Oh, I thought he was a local man?

NORMAN: Dr Killick? No, no, been here about – oh, eighteen months, I should say?

FRAZER: Is that all?

NORMAN: Yes, about eighteen months. But he's a good chap for all that. Seems to put himself out to help folk. Must be pretty well off, I imagine.

FRAZER: Help? In what way, do you mean?

NORMAN: Oh, I don't know. That Miss Hoskins he mentioned just now for instance – two old maids they are; he looks after them like they was children – and by gum, they need it!

FRAZER laughs.

NORMAN: And then again – he's done a lot for Walters, the chap we call Rembrandt.

FRAZER: That's the artist I was hearing about earlier?

NORMAN: That's the one. Toughest looking chap I've ever seen. Lives on a cabin cruiser out on

163

the saltings. Drinks like a fish. Dr Killick's got him out of trouble on more than one occasion. I'm sure of that.

FRAZER: Really?

NORMAN: Aye. And he's bought some of his pictures – to keep him going, like.

Several of the customers seen in the previous scene return to the bar. They are talking among themselves about the darts match. WILL TRUMAN calls over to NORMAN.

WILL: Come along now, Norman! What about some service? Or do you want us all to go back to the Crown?

NORMAN rises and makes for the bar.

NORMAN: (*Smiling*) You can if you like – if you can stomach that stuff they palm off on you as beer over there!

FRAZER puts the photographs and the letter into his pocket. He rises and goes to the bar, standing next to WILL TRUMAN.

FRAZER: How did the match go?

WILL: Rotten! We 'ad a hell of a job to hit the board!

FRAZER: (*Laughing*) It was one of those nights, was it? I know. (*Pleasantly*) Will you have a drink? I'm just getting one.

WILL: Well, I won't say no. I'll have a mild.

FRAZER: One mild, one bitter, please, Norman.

NORMAN: (*Busy*) Coming up!

FRAZER: I heard you talking about Rembrandt earlier on – sounded like a good story. What happened?

WILL: Wasn't much to it, really. We was coming in when we hears this fight going on – so we goes aboard. It wasn't a fight after all, just old Rembrandt – drunk as a lord and breaking up the happy home!

FRAZER: He sounds quite a character!

WILL: He is that!

The telephone at the end of the bar starts ringing just as NORMAN is giving FRAZER and WILL TRUMAN their drinks. NORMAN crosses to the telephone and answers it.

WILL: Good health, Mr Frazer!

FRAZER: Cheers.

FRAZER and WILL TRUMAN drink.

NORMAN: (*At the telephone*) It's for you, Mr Frazer.

FRAZER puts down his drink and crosses to the telephone.

FRAZER: (*To NORMAN*) Is it London?

NORMAN: I don't think so – sounds like a local call.

FRAZER picks up the receiver.

FRAZER: (*On the phone*) Frazer speaking …

CUT TO: A Telephone Box. Evening.

HARRY DENSTON is on the telephone, his face is badly bruised and he has a cut over his right eye. He looks dazed, confused, and unkempt. There is another man in the box with him, a big, fierce looking man. This is WALTERS, known locally as REMBRANDT. WALTERS is supporting HARRY DENSTON by the arm. He is forcing HARRY to make the call.

HARRY: … Tim – this is Harry … If you want to see me, I'll meet you in … about an hour.

CUT TO: The Three Bells. As before.

For the duration of this conversation we cut back and forth between FRAZER and the telephone box.

FRAZER: Where? Harry! Where?

HARRY DENSTON opens his mouth to speak, but is too weak.

165

WALTERS: (*Whispering fiercely*) Tell him!
HARRY tries to rouse himself, but fails to do so and shakes his head. WALTERS grabs him and hurls him out of the box and into the arms of the waiting LESTER.

CUT TO: Evening.
LESTER leads HARRY DENSTON to a car which is parked near the telephone box.

CUT TO: The Telephone Box. Evening.
WALTERS is picking up the dangling receiver. Again, we cut back and forth between the telephone box and FRAZER in the pub.
FRAZER: (*Tensely*) Harry – where can we meet?
WALTERS: I'll see you at the jetty – near the Old Bell.
WALTERS rings off and leaves the box.

CUT TO: The bar of The Three Bells. As before.
FRAZER is still on the telephone.
FRAZER: (*On the phone*) Harry? Harry? Are you there? Harry?
FRAZER realises that HARRY DENSTON has gone. Slowly he replaces the receiver. NORMAN is looking at him.
FRAZER: Norman, what's the "Old Bell"?
NORMAN: The Old Bell? That's the old Ship Bell they got hanging down on the jetty.
FRAZER: I see. Thanks.
FRAZER picks up his drink, finishes it, then with a nod to NORMAN and WILL TRUMAN he walks towards the staircase.

CUT TO: The Jetty at Henton. Night.
The place is deserted and the warehouses cast enormous shadows over the large open space.

166

FRAZER's car drives up and stops outside a small stone business at the end of the jetty. FRAZER gets out and looks about him. In front of the small building we see the old bell suspended from an old fashioned iron wall-bracket. FRAZER sees this and moves over to it. He stops beneath it and looks about him. There is no-one in sight. He takes out a cigarette and lights it, then looks at his watch.

In the shadow of one of the warehouses, we see LESTER watching FRAZER.

FRAZER turns and looks idly in LESTER's direction.

LESTER moves further back into the shadows.

FRAZER then looks keenly towards the warehouse where LESTER is hiding. He sees a slight movement in the shadow of the warehouse, then deliberately moves out a short distance from the small building and turns his back on the warehouse. He waits tensely.

LESTER waits in the shadows then moves forward very slowly and cautiously. As he leaves the shadows he takes a knife from his pocket and flicks open the blade. The blade clicks fairly audibly.

FRAZER hears the knife flick but he does not move.

Over his shoulder we see that LESTER has reached the corner of the small building; he is making his way softly over the last few yards that separate him from FRAZER.

At the last possible moment, FRAZER whirls round on LESTER. LESTER surprised, makes a jump at FRAZER. They fight – silently, except for the sound of heavy breathing.

After a struggle, LESTER is forced to drop the knife and FRAZER kicks it away towards the edge of the jetty.

LESTER breaks away and tries to get the knife. FRAZER grabs him and pulls him up by the coat collar. He hits him hard and LESTER topples over into the sea.

FRAZER stands looking down into the water for a moment, but sees no sign of LESTER. He stoops, picks up the knife, and tosses it into the sea. Then he walks slowly back towards his car.

FRAZER gets into his car and drives away. In the foreground, as he does so, we see the old bell.

CUT TO: Aboard a Cabin Cruiser on the saltings at Henton. Day.

WALTERS comes up the companionway and empties a bucket of trash over the side of the boat. He pauses for a moment to take a breath of fresh air. He notices someone on the quay.

FRAZER is walking slowly along the quay towards the cabin cruiser.

WALTERS takes a good look at FRAZER, then hurries halfway down the companionway: we see over his shoulder into the cabin. HARRY DENSTON is lying on one of the bunks. He looks dazed, and ill: It is obvious that he has recently been beaten up. WALTERS speaks to someone else in the cabin, who remains out of vision.

WALTERS: Keep him quiet! There's someone coming!

CUT TO: Aboard the Cabin Cruiser. Day.

FRAZER arrives opposite the cabin cruiser and crosses the gangplank onto the boat. WALTERS comes up the companionway once more.

WALTERS: (*Belligerently*) What are you after, mister? This is private property!

FRAZER: Mr Walters?

WALTERS: That's me. What do you want?

FRAZER: My name's Clifton. I'm an art dealer. I understand you …

WALTERS: Clifton? I've never heard of you!

168

FRAZER: That's not surprising; I hadn't heard of you
              until a fortnight ago.
WALTERS: Well?
FRAZER: I've been in New York for the past four
              years. Now I'm opening a gallery in New
              Bond Street, and I'm looking for pictures
              with a definite …
WALTERS: (*Suspiciously*) Who told you to come here?
              Who told you about me?
FRAZER: My word, you're a very suspicious
              individual! If you're not interested in selling
              your work, just say so, and I'll go
              elsewhere.
WALTERS: You haven't answered my question!
FRAZER: What was your question?
WALTERS: Who told you about me?
FRAZER: (*Indifferently, turning away*) Oh, forget it,
              my dear fellow! I can't waste my time on
              temperamental …

WALTERS suddenly grabs hold of FRAZER's arm.

WALTERS: (*Pushing his face towards FRAZER's*)
              Answer the question!

FRAZER looks at WALTERS, apparently unperturbed.

FRAZER: Henry Frindale told me about you. I saw a
              picture of yours in his gallery. I liked it and
              he told me where I could get in touch with
              you.
WALTERS: What was it a picture of?
FRAZER: It was a shopping basket on a kitchen table.

WALTERS releases FRAZER's arm.

WALTERS: (*Smiling*) I should think you bloody well did
              like it! It's the best picture you've seen,
              mate, in years!

FRAZER: A slight overstatement, Mr Walters.
              (*Smiling*) However, I must admit it wasn't
              entirely without merit.

FRAZER flicks the sleeve of his overcoat.

FRAZER: Are you working on anything at the
              moment?
WALTERS: I've just finished a picture. (*Impressively*)
              Best thing I've done, I can tell you that
              straight away!
FRAZER: Supposing you let the picture speak for
              itself?
WALTERS: (*Hesitantly, still a shade suspicious*) You
              say Henry Frindale sent you?
FRAZER: (*Shaking his head*) No, I simply saw one of
              your pictures and became interested in you.
WALTERS: But you know Frindale?
FRAZER: (*A shade impatiently*) Of course I know
              him! I know all the dealers. (*A note of
              sarcasm*) Would you prefer that I called
              back later with a letter of introduction?
WALTERS: No, don't be a fathead – of course not!
FRAZER: Then I suggest you let me see the picture.
              Who knows? We may be wasting my time
              as well as yours.

*WALTERS stares at FRAZER, annoyed – then suddenly he
gives a nod and moves towards the companionway.*

WALTERS: I'll fetch it.

*WALTERS disappears down the companionway again.
FRAZER looks about him as unobtrusively as possible. He
sees a lifebelt hanging on the superstructure of the cabin
and moves round to have a closer look at it. We see his face
register surprise as he stares at it. The name of the cabin
cruiser is inscribed on the lifebelt. It is called "ANYA".*

End of Episode Six

Episode Seven

OPEN TO: The Cabin Cruiser. Day.

FRAZER is on the deck of the cabin cruiser, staring at the name "Anya" on the lifebelt. He turns and looks at the companionway leading to the cabin below.

CUT TO: Inside The Cabin Cruiser. Day.

Walters is sorting out some of his canvases, which are stacked against one of the walls. He is talking to a man who is out of vision.

WALTERS: I tell you this chap's a dealer – a genuine dealer. Old Henry Frindale sent him down here.

As WALTERS speaks the camera pans to show HARRY DENSTON lying on the bunk with DR KILLICK standing by his side, looking down at him.

KILLICK: (*Annoyed*) I don't care who he is! I don't want people calling here! I've told you that often enough!

WALTERS: (*Angrily*) Look, clever Dr Killick! I've got a right to sell my pictures here or anywhere else I like! I do your dirty work looking after him (*Pointing to DENSTON*) and keeping the swine quiet! So I sell my pictures when and where I please, see!

KILLICK: (*Moving towards WALTERS*) Look, don't stand here arguing like a fishwife! Show your friend what he wants to see, and then get rid of him!

WALTERS: (*Surely, turning towards one of his canvases*) He's no friend of mine.

KILLICK: (*Surprised*) You mean you don't know him?

WALTERS: No, I've never seen him before.

KILLICK: Then how the hell do you know he's a dealer?

175

WALTERS: (*Impatiently*) I told you, Frindale sent him! He's a dealer all right – I can smell 'em a mile off.

KILLICK gives WALTERS an angry look and moves towards the door.

KILLICK: I think I'd better take a look at this gentleman.

KILLICK goes up the companionway a few steps and peers out.

CUT TO: The Cabin Cruiser. Day.

From KILLICK's eyeline we see FRAZER looking out towards the quay.

KILLICK, in a rage, goes back down the steps into the cabin.

CUT TO: Inside The Cabin Cruiser. Day. As before.

KILLICK: You damn fool! You idiot! That's the man I told you about – Frazer!

WALTERS: (*Turning*) Frazer?

KILLICK: Get rid of him! Get him off my boat! Do you hear what I say – get rid of him!

HARRY DENSTON, who has heard all this, looks up when the name of FRAZER is mentioned. Suddenly, he raises himself on one elbow, and shouts with all the strength he can muster.

HARRY: Tim! Tim!

CUT TO: The Cabin Cruiser. Day.

FRAZER hears the shout, and quickly turns towards the cabin. There is another shout from below.

CUT TO: Inside The Cabin Cruiser. Day. As before.
WALTERS and KILLICK are struggling with HARRY
DENSTON: trying to keep him quiet. KILLICK hits him
across the face and HARRY falls back onto the bunk, semi-
conscious.
KILLICK: Stay with Denston! Stay with him while I
               try to get rid of Frazer! And for God's sake
               keep him quiet!
KILLICK picks up his bag from the table and goes up the
companionway.

CUT TO: The Cabin Cruiser. Day.
FRAZER, on the deck, is moving towards the
companionway. KILLICK comes up on deck. He sees
FRAZER and walks towards him, smiling.
KILLICK: Why, Mr Frazer! What are you doing here?
FRAZER: (*Unsmiling*) What's more to the point –
               what are you doing here, doctor?
KILLICK: I have a patient on board – he's delirious.
               You may have heard the commotion.
FRAZER: Yes, I heard someone shouting, if that's
               what you mean. Who is your patient?
KILLICK: (*Affably*) He's a relation of Rembrandt's.
               (*With a little laugh*) Forgive me, I mean
               Walters. But of course, you don't know
               Walters, do you? He's an artist, amongst
               other things.
FRAZER: And you, Dr Killick, are a liar!
KILLICK: (*Astonished*) I beg your pardon?
FRAZER: You're a liar, Killick! Your patient isn't a
               relative of Rembrandt. (*Quietly, looking at*
               KILLICK) He's Harry Denston …

177

KILLICK: Harry Denston? My dear fellow, I really
             think you've got that friend of yours on the
             brain! You don't really think …

FRAZER moves towards the companionway.

KILLICK: Where do you think you're going?

FRAZER: I'll give you three guesses!

KILLICK: (*Annoyed*) My patient can't be disturbed! I
             forbid you to go down there, do you
             understand?

FRAZER: (*Interrupting KILLICK*) Killick, your
             patient is Harry Denston!

FRAZER takes a revolver out of his pocket.

FRAZER: Now stop bluffing – and tell Walters to
             bring him up on deck.

KILLICK stares at the revolver.

KILLICK: Are you threatening me?

FRAZER: (*Nodding*) Yes, I'm threatening you,
             Killick! By God, I'm threatening you! Now
             do as I say; tell Rembrandt to bring him up
             on deck!

*KILLICK, frightened now, hesitates for a moment, then he
turns his head towards the cabin and calls down.*

KILLICK: Rembrandt! Bring Denston up here!

*FRAZER automatically looks towards the cabin for a
moment as KILLICK calls. As he does so, KILLICK takes
advantage of the situation and knocks FRAZER's gun out of
his hand with his bag. The gun slithers to the other side of
the deck.*

*KILLICK breaks away and races for the gangplank on the
other side of the boat. FRAZER dives for his gun, picks it
up, and is about to fire at the retreating KILLICK, when he
checks himself and aims the gun vertically into the air,
firing twice.*

KILLICK is by now on the quay and racing for the shelter of a side street. He has almost reached it when two police cars turn round the corner and stop. Several plain-clothes men jump out of the cars and head him off.

KILLICK stops in his tracks, then doubles back the way he has come. Another two police cars pull up on that side, however, cutting him off. The men on both sides advance towards him.

KILLICK now realises that he is trapped; he turns and stares with hatred at FRAZER on the cruiser.

On the deck of the cabin cruiser FRAZER stands, his revolver ready, facing the companionway.

WALTERS comes up the steps, sees FRAZER's gun, and raises his hands. We see several policemen, headed by CAXTON, coming across the gangplank onto the boat.

FRAZER: (*To the policemen*) All right – take this one.

FRAZER goes down the companionway.

Two policemen grab WALTERS and start to march him off the boat. CAXTON turns towards the companionway.

CUT TO: Inside The Cabin Cruiser. Day.

FRAZER is lifting HARRY DENSTON from the floor. As he gets him onto the bunk, HARRY clutches at FRAZER's arm.

HARRY: (*Weakly*) I'm sorry, Tim … I … dragged you … into … all this.

FRAZER produces a hip flask and opens it. He lifts HARRY's head and pours a little of the liquid down his throat.

FRAZER: Come on – drink this … You can talk later, Harry. You've got all the time in the world now.

CUT TO: Outside FRAZER's Flat. The next morning.
A taxi drives up and DONALD EDWARDS gets out of it; he pays off the driver and walks towards the entrance to FRAZER's flat.

CUT TO: FRAZER's Drawing Room. Day.
As the doorbell rings, FRAZER puts down the print of the North Star he is holding. He goes out into the hall.

CUT TO: The Hall of FRAZER's Flat. Day.
FRAZER opens the front door.
FRAZER: Ah, Mr Edwards! Come along in! It was nice of you to call.
EDWARDS enters the flat.
FRAZER: How's your wife? What's the latest news?
EDWARDS: She's off the danger list now. They say she should be up and about in four or five weeks.
FRAZER: Good. I'm delighted to hear that. Please go through.

CUT TO: FRAZER's Drawing Room. Day.
FRAZER and EDWARDS enter.
FRAZER: Do sit down, Mr Edwards.
EDWARDS hesitates for a moment, looks at FRAZER, then sits in the armchair.
EDWARDS: Thank you.
FRAZER: I expect you're wondering why I asked you to call?
EDWARDS: Well, I am a little puzzled, I must confess.
FRAZER: I want to tell you a story, Mr Edwards.
FRAZER sits on the arm of the settee, facing EDWARDS.
FRAZER: I feel sure it will interest you. It concerns the North Star.

180

EDWARDS: The North Star?

FRAZER: That's right. Not a very pretty story, really, but I think you'll be intrigued by it.

EDWARDS: (*Looking at his watch*) I haven't a lot of time, you know.

FRAZER: Oh, you've time enough for this. It also concerns a friend of mine called Harry Denston.

EDWARDS: Harry Denston? I've heard that name before.

FRAZER: You have indeed. You used the North Star as a stepping-stone to get to know Harry and to gain his confidence. He bought some old maritime prints.

Showing EDWARDS the print he was holding.

FRAZER: This was one of them.

EDWARDS: I think there must be some mistake, Mr Frazer. The first time I saw this print was when you brought it to the cottage. (*Smiling; shaking his head*) And I most certainly don't know this friend of yours – Denston?

FRAZER: I think you do. You see, I have this story on the very best authority.

EDWARDS: What authority?

FRAZER: Your half-brother – Dr Killick – Anya's father.

EDWARDS: (*After a moment: quietly*) Go on …

FRAZER: You built Harry a model of the North Star using this print as a guide. When you got to know Harry better, and discovered he was in financial difficulties, you offered him money to photograph a certain formula. Harry agreed to do what you wanted. (*Shaking his head*) But he didn't play it

181

straight, Mr Edwards. He double-crossed you and gave you a microfilm containing false information.

EDWARDS: Go on, Mr Frazer …

FRAZER: Harry then contacted an East German organisation and arranged to meet their representative, Anstrov, at Henton. You heard about this and immediately informed them that Denston hadn't got the formula and that you were the man to contact. You kidnapped Denston and tried to make him talk, but all you could get out of him was that the microfilm was in the North Star. You sent your friend Lester to get the ship from Harry's flat. When he arrived he saw Crombie leaving – with it under his arm. Lester followed him back here – murdered him – and took the ship.

EDWARDS: (*Without thinking*) But the film wasn't in it!

FRAZER: No – it wasn't. But when Harry told you it was in the North Star he was telling you the truth. The film <u>was</u> in the North Star – but not in the ship!

FRAZER picks up the print again and puts it face down on the table. He removes the backing and takes out an envelope. He opens the envelope and extracts a length of film.

FRAZER: You were so convinced that Harry meant the ship that it never occurred to you to look in the print!

EDWARDS suddenly rises to his feet. He puts his hand in his pocket and takes out a revolver. He moves towards FRAZER; his hand on the trigger of the revolver.

FRAZER stares. It is obvious that EDWARDS is going to fire. Suddenly Frazer moves forward and simultaneous with FRAZER's movement there is the sound of a revolver shot.

For a split second the two men stand facing each other then EDWARDS' arm drops and he slumps forward.

The camera pans to the entrance to the bedroom where HOBSON is standing in the doorway, holding a revolver. It is still pointing at DONALD EDWARDS.

CUT TO: The Library at Molton Square. Day.

ROSS is sitting at his desk talking to FRAZER who is sitting on the other side of it.

ROSS: … All things considered, it was a good thing we'd arranged for Hobson to be at your flat when you saw Edwards. Outwardly, Edwards may have appeared as a meek little man, nevertheless he was indirectly responsible for the deaths of Crombie and Tupper. (*He lights a cigarette*) Incidentally, did Edwards find out about that note his wife sent you? Is that why he tried to kill her?

FRAZER: No, he heard her talking to me on the telephone, and he thought I was doing a private deal with her over the film.

ROSS: Then he thought you had the film?

FRAZER: Yes, he thought Harry might have passed it on to me. Funny, really – because I had the film when I had the print, but I didn't know it!

ROSS: (*Nodding*) Edwards obviously didn't know which way to turn. First he thought it might be in Harry's car, then he concentrated on the ship …

183

FRAZER:	(*Interrupting ROSS; nodding*) Yes, that's why they wanted the photograph. When they found the film wasn't in it they thought someone must have switched the ships. A photograph would have shown Edwards any little differences.
ROSS:	I understand you saw Mrs Edwards this morning?
FRAZER:	Yes, and she explained about the note. Apparently two men came over from East Germany; Anstrov and …
ROSS:	(*Interrupting FRAZER: smiling*) Anstrov and Nikiyan. Anstrov was the important man and Nikiyan his assistant. They changed names and identities as a security measure. It was Nikiyan who died.
FRAZER:	And Anstrov?
ROSS:	He left for Berlin this morning.
FRAZER:	(*Surprised*) You let him go?
ROSS:	Yes.
FRAZER:	Why?
ROSS:	If we'd picked him up there would have been complications. We like to avoid complications as much as possible. Our job was to see that he left empty-handed. (*Nodding*) He did, Mr Frazer.
FRAZER:	What happens to Harry Denston now?
ROSS:	I don't know, it's out of my hands. The Home Secretary's got the details, it's up to him now, I'm afraid. (*Smiling*) But I'm more concerned about what happens to you.
FRAZER:	What do you mean?
ROSS:	What are you going to do now this business is over?

FRAZER:	I don't know. I've had an offer of a job in Australia, but I'm not really keen on it.
ROSS:	An engineering job?
FRAZER:	Yes: in Perth.

ROSS looks at FRAZER: he continues to smoke his cigarette.

ROSS:	How would you like to work for me, Frazer?
FRAZER:	You mean – permanently? Join your department?
ROSS:	(*Nodding*) Yes; that's what I mean. I'm offering you Crombie's job.

FRAZER looks at ROSS for a moment.

FRAZER:	I'd like that; I'd like that very much.
ROSS:	Good. Be back in this office by six o'clock and I'll tell you about Barbara Day and the Salinger affair.
FRAZER:	The Salinger affair?
ROSS:	(*Nodding*) Yes …
FRAZER:	What's the Salinger affair?
ROSS:	It's your next assignment. Come back at six o'clock and I'll introduce you to a colleague of mine and tell you all about it …

THE END

But when televised, Episode Seven continued here with the opening scenes of *The World of Tim Frazer – The Salinger Affair*, to be published in this series in 2023 by Williams & Whiting

Press Pack
press cuttings about *The World of Tim Frazer* ...

Durbridge Thriller For TV by Cathryn Rose
Francis Durbridge, creator of that famous amateur detective
Paul Temple, thinks he may have created the tv equivalent
in Tim Frazer, central character in an 18-week BBC thriller
series which begins on November 15.

Such a long serial is a new departure for Durbridge, but
he explained to me that it is divided into three separate
stories running consecutively.

Durbridge, a round, balding, rather shy man, looks more
like a rather nervy Hatton Garden jeweller than a writer of
sinister detective yarns.

He created Paul Temple in 1937, and since then has
been in unquenchable demand as a writer of radio – and
latterly – tv mysteries.

Durbridge is a Yorkshireman by birth, lives now in
Weybridge, Surrey, where he works "office hours" on his
writing.

He is married and has two sons aged 19 and 12.

The plum part of Tim Frazer goes to a young actor
called Jack Hedley who already has an established and
admiring "clientele."

His most noticeable recent tv appearance was as a young
Midlands salesman, in London for his firm's party, who gets
tight and manages to salvage a joke about a wife and a
jaguar from his drunken stupor.

Another memorable performance of his was as Corp in
No Fixed Abode, the story of four men in a dosshouse.

Jack, a tall, good-looking, fair-haired bachelor of 30,
says: "I often play Northerners – Liverpudlians, or
Scotsmen – and I'm usually a schizo or a mental defective
or an inarticulate lover or a bum of some sort."

In fact, Jack is a rather upper-class young man – ex-public-school son of a wealthy mother who founded and runs a successful advertising business.

He joined the Navy from school, bent on making it his career, and stayed eight years until he was invalided out after taking part in the Korean war.

He went into the family business, but couldn't stand that, so went along to R.A.D.A.

"There were 350 applicants for 50 places and I managed to get one of them."

In *The World of Tim Frazer* Jack plays a sophisticated young man with a mews house and a Jaguar car and nice clothes.

In real life Jack is a little like this. He has a flat in Mayfair and runs a big, sporty, convertible car.

He studies Egyptology in his spare time and likes reading books on political history.

Leicester Evening Mail

New Francis Durbridge Series

Tim Frazer is the central character in the three adventure stories which form the new Francis Durbridge series – *The World of Tim Frazer* on BBC television.

There are three separate adventures, not a continuous story, in this 18-week series – the first of its kind. The first story starts on Tuesday, November 15, and the part of Tim Frazer is played by Jack Hedley.

Tim Frazer used to be an engineer, but his business has collapsed and left him without a job. In the first story he decides to look up his old friend and business partner, Harry Denston, in the fishing village of Henton.

Durbridge addicts will know that peaceful surroundings can provide a contrasting background for sensational happenings.

188

Although a Yorkshireman by birth, Francis Durbridge has spent most of his life in London and the Midlands. He has a long list of sound broadcasting scripts to his credit including, of course, the Paul Temple serials.

The last of his eight television serials, *The Scarf*, was seen in March 1959.

Jack Hedley (Tim Frazer) has, since he left the R.A.D.A. in 1957, packed in a great deal of experience in films, theatre and television. His first BBC tv broadcast was in an episode of *Fair Game* in 1958. One of his most successful performances was in *Mine Own Executioner* in 1959.

Ralph Michael, who also plays a leading part, has appeared in many BBC tv productions, from *Mourning Becomes Electra* in 1947 to *Julius Caesar* this year.

Brighton Gazette

Successor To Paul Temple by **Peter Jackson**

Francis Durbridge will always be associated with the Paul Temple serials, which established his reputation on sound radio. But since then he has spread his net to include television and to capture a new audience, most of whom are unashamedly Durbridge addicts.

His work has a smoothness and slickness which is irreproachable and yet he spurns the cheap tricks of his trade which attempt to hide the identity of the criminals by false clues.

His characters are plausible and his situations possible. If there is a tendency for his villains to be of the blackest and his heroes to be spotless, that is excusable.

The last Durbridge television serial we saw (there have been eight of them in all) was *The Scarf* which was shown in the early part of last year. This was a model of television serial writing which has been copied with varying degrees of success.

Perhaps Durbridge's greatest claim to fame is that he has established the pattern of crime serials not only for the BBC but for ITV as well.

His latest work for BBC television is a set of three serials planned to cover an eighteen-week period. They will all deal with one character, Tim Frazer, played by Jack Hedley. The first episode of *The World of Tim Frazer* is on November 15.

Yorkshire Post

Author Takes Stock of Tim Frazer

Full marks to Francis Durbridge for saying categorically of his new BBC tv character, Tim Frazer: "He is not a private eye."

This from the celebrated author of goodness knows how many Paul Temple series is a stimulating statement.

I imagine that, thanks to the absorbent qualities of the most colossal sponge in the world – television – pretty well all the changes on detectives, dicks, busies, rozzers and private eyes have been rung.

It is a sensible departure to recognise the fact that an ordinary, pleasant, likeable character – for this is what I think we will find Frazer to be – can just as easily be caught in adventures – adventures strong enough to form the basis for three separate stories in an 18-week series.

Durbridge makes his new character an engineer who started a small machine tool business of his own which went broke. His partner disappeared, owing our hero some money, and it is in pursuit of this missing cash that he comes up against strange happenings.

Tim Frazer is to be played by Jack Hedley.

Western Evening Herald

Any new series by Francis Durbridge – the Yorkshire-born creator of Paul Temple and Steve – is to be welcomed, and tonight (BBC, 8pm) introduces *The World of Tim Frazer*, a new character.

Durbridge has gone up in the world since he first started writing thrillers, and as an executive producer doesn't get all the time he might for writing.

So in this series he had two script associates, well-known television playwrights Clive Exton and Barry Thomas, helping, as well as novelist Charles Hatton.

What is it to be? Many hands make light work? Or too many cooks? I think that with his vast experience Durbridge is onto another winner.

Tim Frazer, played by Jack Hedley, is a former engineer whose business has collapsed and left him without a job. A happy-go-lucky sort of fellow, he irritates you and at the same time charms. And when he arrives at the oh-so-peaceful fishing village of Henton, the action starts.

Yorkshire Evening Press

Dial Tim

Francis Durbridge, creator of radio's Paul Temple, presents a new character in his series *The World of Tim Frazer* (BBC 8pm).

Tim (Jack Hedley) is described by the author as "a product of a minor English public school, a much-travelled bachelor of thirty-five with plenty of charm."

He will NOT be "a tough, violent character, with a mid-Atlantic accent," says Durbridge.

He adds: "If violence occurs it will be the inevitable development of the story itself."

The series is an experiment to find out whether bachelor Tim can become, in vision, the success Temple has been in sound.

In tonight's episode, Tim goes to a northern fishing village to seek out a missing business partner.

He meets a dying Russian who can only mutter a girl's name – "Anya."

Daily Mirror

Now The BBC Try Tim In His Own World

Francis Durbridge is one of those rare televisions writers who can rely almost solely on his name and reputation to attract a sizeable first-night following.

And he comes to the BBC screen again tonight additionally strengthened by the fact that his last serial *The Scarf* still echoes pleasantly in the memories of many viewers.

But apart from this hopeful anticipation, the new Durbridge series *The World of Tim Frazer* is a very much wait-and-see affair.

Durbridge says of his hero Tim: "He is not a tough, gimmicky, trigger-happy, dame-slapping, mid-Atlantic character of no fixed abode."

He is ordinary enough to have been an engineer – "rather like the chap you met the other day" – says the author.

First setting is the peaceful fishing village of Henton where Tim is visiting an old business partner. And we may be assured that rural life will spark up when Jack Hedley, who plays Tim, sets foot on the scene.

Southern Evening Echo

Tonight by Malcolm Moore

Everything seems to add up to eighteen Tuesday nights of worthwhile BBC tv viewing in this new Francis Durbridge thriller series *The World of Tim Frazer*. Durbridge, of course, is to tv and radio what Agatha Christie is to the novel – master of the unexpected twist. He did the Paul Temple stories for radio and most recently, *The Scarf* for tv. The new series has an unusual arrangement in being divided into three separate six-part tales starring Jack Hedley in the name role.

Manchester Evening Chronicle

This Thriller Will Give Jack A Thin Time
by **James Green**

The World of Tim Frazer, the most ambitious thriller-serial yet presented by BBC tv starts tonight (8.0) and can be seen for the next 18 Tuesdays.

It is a big break for actor Jack Hedley to be asked to play Frazer – an engineer who suddenly becomes involved with security and M.I.5.

As Tim Frazer's world gets peak-hour showing and scripts by Francis Durbridge and Clive Exton, the BBC reckon rightly, that Mr Hedley is a lucky fellow.

He has repaid the Corporation by voluntarily going on a diet. Which means that Tim Frazer today is one and a half stones lighter than he was five weeks ago.

The diet? No sugar, alcohol, fruit or salt. But steak, chicken, fish and fresh vegetables are allowed.

Said Hedley: "The worst part is the boredom of eating the same dishes and explaining to friends why I'm not drinking."

Now that he's well under twelve stone he thinks the effort has been worthwhile.

The Durbridge story – or rather stories, for there are three serials each of six episodes – is the usual clue-strewn battle of wits involving viewers.

Evening News

Durbridge Up To His Old Tricks

Francis Durbridge, I suppose one might say, is to the television serial, what Edgar Wallace was to the detective novel. Wallace had, and Durbridge has, the gift of creating and manipulating characters with great skill.

At times this kind of writing suggests almost an assembly line technique, producing a glossy, acceptable, but not particularly high-quality end product.

A new Durbridge serial, *The World of Tim Frazer*, started on BBC television last night. Episode One, that treacherous trap for the unwary critic, seemed to be well up to the standard. All the old tricks were there, fast moving action, foreign accents, a blonde charmer, a bloke from M.I.5. and meaning looks by the dozen.

My wife is a great Durbridge enthusiast. She says she likes these serials because she always knows exactly what is going to happen next.

Liverpool Daily Post

The BBC's *The World of Tim Frazer* got away to a crisp, enjoyable start last night.

The settings are excellent, the Durbridge dialogue is natural in the best dramatic way, and Jack Hedley's Tim, a sad-eyed no-nonsense feller, is suitably engaging.

I was particularly impressed by the way direction and acting dealt with the various scene climaxes.

No blaze of music, expressions of horror, gasped exclamations. But a thoughtful appraisal by Tim of the situation and a response to it in the way which we would like to think would be our own.

Southern Evening Echo

194

Tenterhooks Coming Up

A new serial from Francis Durbridge is an event as exciting to the discerning viewer as a new style from Paris to the discerning woman. Elegance, good taste and craftsmanship can always be found.

The World of Tim Frazer written by Mr Durbridge in collaboration this time with Clive Exton, began with superb confidence and polish, and with enough mystery and promise of excitement to keep one on the tenterest of hooks. Jack Hedley as Mr Frazer makes a most gentlemanly hero and his efforts to find the elusive Harry Denston will undoubtedly be rewarded. So, too, will the viewers who follow him. The only peccadillo last night was committed by security man Ross (Ralph Michael) who failed to secure a lighted cigarette.

Looking In Last Night

When the BBC mounted its new Tim Frazer tv series, pre-publicity promised that it would not be another private-eye series. There would be no slugging and no gun-play.

Remarkably, the promise was kept last night in the first instalment, which showed that Francis Durbridge, creator of Paul Temple, still had the master's touch for creating serialising suspense. And, not only is Frazer not a clean-limbed American detective, he is easily identifiable as British. That in itself is worth something on tv these days.

Oldham Evening Chronicle and Standard

His Eyelids Fit Like Safe-Doors by **Richard Sear**

Back to the BBC bringing a bump of suspense came writer Francis Durbridge last night with a new series *The World of Tim Frazer* … Rather I should say a new character, played by Jack Hedley and said to be "a product of a minor English public school."

Mr Hedley, whose eyelids fit like safe doors, put over Tim Frazer as if he were a product of a major English public school – say, Eton.

He got himself involved with a dying Russian seaman, the Intelligence side of the Civil Service, and a mysterious child, without much more than a non-committal grunt.

As with all tv bachelors, he had a faintly blousy girlfriend whom he treated as if she were an antique vase.

I think I am going to like Mr Hedley – although the name is faintly redolent of soap powder – he is so far removed from the usual type who seizes a woman with one arm and a crook with the other.

Perhaps he will turn into another Paul Temple – which is what the BBC/Durbridge axis is hoping for. And why not?

Certainly Tim Frazer is going to be a pin-up boy before he is finished, and give us some smooth suspense.

I was sorry that in this live programme the Civil Servant dropped his cigarette and fluffed his lines; it slightly cracked the tense atmosphere.

Daily Mirror

Master of Mystery by **Roy Wilson** (contains spoilers)
A new Francis Durbridge serial on BBC Television is always a special occasion, for he is a writer who has never let us down. His latest, *The World of Tim Frazer* is extra special, because it is three serials in one, three separate adventures in eighteen episodes – enough Durbridge mystery and excitement, in fact, to last us until the middle of next March.

Mr Durbridge has worked on these three serials with other writers: Clive Exton, Barry Thomas and Charles Hatton. In last night's first episode there was no sign of a dividing-line between Durbridge and Exton – a young tv playwright who has made a strong impression with his

Armchair Theatre scripts – but I have no doubt it will prove to be a fruitful collaboration.

The first instalment had the true Durbridge stamp all right, particularly in the closing scene, when Tim Frazer discovers that the Anya whose name was on a dying Russian seaman's lips was (apparently) a little girl living in a country cottage.

Tim Frazer, played by Jack Hedley – an excellent piece of casting – is the quiet, manly, dogged type of hero who has woman-appeal while remaining thoroughly masculine. I think we shall find him an engaging fellow. At the behest of a secret Government department that has "unlimited funds" (it must be of a rare importance) he is off on the trail of a man who owes him money and appears to be mixed up somehow with the Russians.

An intriguing beginning. I shall be surprised if it does not turn out well.

Eastern Evening News

Watching a Francis Durbridge serial gives a pleasure comparable with reading a good book or taking a walk in the springtime. So refreshing.

It was apparent in the first few minutes that his association with Clive Exton on the script of *The World of Tim Frazer* had not robbed the story of an expertly woven plot. Exton also has a flair for character building, which helps.

The mark of Durbridge is that the drama gets on with the tale, appears uncomfortably real, and develops to an unexpected cliffhanger situation at the end of each episode.

Manchester Evening Chronicle

A New Serial Welcomed by **John Willoughby**

Next to plays there are few types of programme as popular as the serial – which no doubt explains why there are eight running at the moment.

The eight does not include established "institutions" such as *Emergency-Ward 10*, *The Larkins*, or *Dixon of Dock Green* which are as much a part of television as *Mrs Dale's Diary* and *The Archers* are of sound radio.

But it does include all the thriller serials which have been joined this week by a distinguished BBC newcomer – Francis Durbridge's *The World of Tim Frazer*.

Judging by the opening session – it runs to 18 episodes – Durbridge, creator of Paul Temple, has lost none of his skill in the art of suspense-building.

This time, however, he is receiving some help. As executive producer of the series Durbridge found his writing time restrictive and was given a collaborator – none other than Clive Exton, who during the last year or two has achieved steadily increasing success with a number of "human" plays on ITV.

The partnership seems ideal and Durbridge is also showing talent as a producer, for in addition to the usual BBC professionalism *The World of Tim Frazer* is a first-class example of film editing.

One of the main weaknesses of American thrillers is the amount of time wasted.

When the hero picks up the phone and says: "I'll be right over," we spend the next five minutes watching him back his limousine out of the garage, light a cigarette, and practically every detail of the journey. Meanwhile, the plot is suspended.

Durbridge allows none of this nonsense to get in the way of his story; every line of dialogue and every action contributes something to the plot. The first episode had

198

enough "meat" in it to fill two episodes of most other serials.

Tim Frazer, a young businessman, was recruited by M.I.5. to trace a missing colleague (the Russians are involved somewhere) is played with Dirk Bogarderish charm by Jack Hedley, who has risen to the top as an actor almost as fast as Clive Exton has as a dramatist.

Oxford Mail

Don't Miss This Episode Tonight by **Ivor Jay**

Heavily underlined televiewing date for tonight is "DON'T miss the second episode of *The World of Tim Frazer*" (BBC 8.0)

That first episode gathered tensions and queries with the adroitness of a galvanic tax-collector doing his nut to reap the Government's lolly from some nimble character about to skip the country.

There was a beautiful economy of dialogue. Meaningful looks.

Swift direction that plunged viewers slap-bang into a mystery that is set sinister to be a good spy yarn. Acting all round was first-rate and Jack Hedley is obviously going to be absolutely fine as husky Tim.

If the standard is maintained we're going to enjoy some delightful and apprehensive escapism. Francis Durbridge, with collaboration from Clive Exton, writes again. For which, many thanks.

Birmingham Evening News

This Sleuth Is Not So Suave by **James Price**

In the second instalment of the thriller serial, *The World of Tim Frazer*, Frazer began to take shape as a character.

Without the suave professionalism of Maigret and his type, he is rather annoyed at being obliged to be a sleuth and I am beginning to take to his sullenness and petulance.

I like the way Francis Durbridge and Clive Exton manage to distill so much mystery out of the small talk of the characters.

All the clues are laid in the idle chatting like that in the seaside pub last week, or in the talk with Mr Edwards, the model builder, this week and the typical haggling over the price of Frazer's car.

Small talk is no weakness in this case. The minor characters that Frazer comes across in his search for his missing friend Harry are all well drawn.

Frazer is certainly allowed to waste no time in between tracking down clues. We were forced to follow him quickly from a cottage to a West End club and then away again to a tumbledown suburban garage.

Meanwhile, hints piled up relentlessly in Mr Frazer's rather ordinary world until the last shot exploded in violence. A man fell into Frazer's arms with a dagger in his back.

That will keep me on edge until next week.

Western Mail

The World of Tim Frazer becomes more and more mysterious and exciting. I had almost dismissed the second instalment of the Francis Durbridge serial as interesting but routine when it blazed into action with a secret service man gasping out a vital message (vague and mysterious, of course) before dying with a knife in his back.

And that was our lot, too, so roll on next Tuesday!

Glasgow Evening Times

The World of Tim Frazer maintained in the second episode, the promise of the first, giving one the pleasant sensation of being slightly concerned in a mystery which someone else can be relied on to solve. Thus one enjoys the titillation without the expenditure of effort – a phrase which sums up most televiewing.

Bolton Evening News

The World of Tim Frazer is warming up and the first blood-stained dagger protruding from a dead man's back made its appearance on Tuesday. I expect to see at least one corpse per instalment from now on.

I rather like Jack Hedley's timing as the leading man. He brings in more halts and pauses in the dialogue than any other "whodunnit" actor I have seen so far. It probably makes producer Alan Bromly tear his hair at times but provided the audience can stick it. I think it makes for a certain realism.

Western Evening Herald

Again The BBC Leaves The Opposition Behind
by **Denis Thomas**

The new Francis Durbridge serial, *The World of Tim Frazer*, is shaping up nicely. We had to wait till the second instalment for a body, but now things are moving along at a spanking pace.

Durbridge has a talent for meaningful irrelevance that never fails to leave its mark. The business of the model ship, the North Star, is of this kind.

Melodramatic? Certainly, but if it tightens up the tension it must be doing its job.

Once again it is worth noting the care and craftsmanship which the BBC lavish on their serials.

This kind of drama is, if anything, even more in need of style than a straight tv theatre production that can be wrapped up in a single sitting. Aware of this, the BBC leaves no rough edges.

Daily Mail

Smooth Thrills by **Richard Sear**

The World of Tim Frazer entered its fourth episode on the BBC last night and there was not a dull moment.

Frazer could not put one foot forward without getting a mysterious message or cock an ear without a telephone jangling.

Suspense piled up like flood water – and yet there were no guns or direct violence.

Writer Francis Durbridge's approach to crime makes the "Philip Marlowe" type of thriller, with its beatings-up, look amateurish.

Jack Hedley gave another excellent performance as an alert Frazer, always prepared for trouble.

Daily Mirror

The World of Tim Frazer thumps along excitedly leaving us each week slightly more bewildered by the wealth of suspicious characters. "See you Monday, not Tuesday," is, no doubt, a common response to invitations these days.

Nottingham Evening News

After four episodes, I'm no nearer solving the problems that beset *The World of Tim Frazer*. I'm beginning to have grave doubts that Francis Durbridge himself knows how it's going to finish! Still, it's one of the best serial thrillers we've had.

Glasgow Sunday Post

Printed in Great Britain
by Amazon

50783868R00128